They hadn't cornered Bolan yet

But it could happen if he didn't stay ahead of them. Step one was blacking out the light, before it marked his place and someone on the sidelines made a lucky shot.

He saw the glaring beam wash over his position, even though it couldn't find him in the shadow of the small communications hut. It wouldn't take the sentries long to close around him, pin him down. Numbers could defeat him then.

He wasn't Superman, wasn't invincible. A storm of fire would drop him where he stood.

Unless he found a way out of the trap.

MACK BOLAN ®
The Executioner

The Executioner®
Don Pendleton's®
DUAL ACTION

A GOLD EAGLE BOOK FROM
WORLDWIDE®

TORONTO • NEW YORK • LONDON
AMSTERDAM • PARIS • SYDNEY • HAMBURG
STOCKHOLM • ATHENS • TOKYO • MILAN
MADRID • WARSAW • BUDAPEST • AUCKLAND

First edition May 2006
ISBN 0-373-64330-6

Special thanks and acknowledgment to
Mike Newton for his contribution to this work.

DUAL ACTION

Printed in U.S.A.

The fires of hate, compressed within the heart,
Burn fiercer and will break at last in flame.
> —Pierre Corneille 1606-1684
> *Le Cid*

I'm fighting fire with fire this time. The risk is that
the end result may be scorched earth.
> —Mack Bolan

To Kofi Annan, Secretary-General of the United Nations.

Blessed are the peacemakers.

Prologue

"Jeez, you get a load of that one?" Eddie Sawyer asked.

"There's nothin' wrong with my eyes," Joe DeLuca answered from the shotgun seat beside him. "Twenty-ten, last time I read the chart."

"So, what's the score, Hawk-eye?"

"I'd give her six."

"I bet you would," Sawyer quipped, "if you had the six to spare."

He tried to get another quick glimpse of the blond hitchhiker in his right-hand mirror, but the armored truck was rolling at a steady 60 mph, and her form had dwindled to the size of a toy soldier in the glass.

"I'm sayin' I've seen better," DeLuca said.

"Not today, you haven't."

"Well—"

"Let's ask the mole." Sawyer reached back and keyed the intercom that linked the driver's section of the truck with the cargo vault behind. "Hey, Tommy boy!" he called. "You see that sweet young thing?"

Tom Nelson's scratchy voice came back at Sawyer through the speaker. "Screw the botha youse."

It was a running joke among the men of Truck 13, Ohio Armored Transport. Nelson's line of vision from the vault was strictly limited, and it was well-known that he spent his travel time immersed in *Popular Mechanics*, trying to "improve" himself. He never saw the sweet young things at roadside, standing with their thumbs out, and a good deal more besides. They always asked him, though, and his reply was perfectly predictable within a narrow range.

Screw you.

Piss off.

Blow me.

The Nelson repertoire.

It never failed—and always got a laugh out of DeLuca.

"Never mind there, Tommy. Sorry I disturbed you," Sawyer offered in meek apology before switching off the intercom.

During the spring and summer months, girl watching was a principal diversion for the men of Truck 13. Of course, they lost the female scenery in autumn, and they saw no one at all on foot during their long runs in the winter. It got boring in a hurry, then, with nothing to watch out for but the black ice on the highway, waiting for a chance to put them in a ditch.

Their long run, once a week, was back and forth from Dayton to Columbus, with a stop in Springfield on the eastbound leg. It wasn't all that far, really—no more than fifty miles—but it seemed longer with the load they had to escort over open country.

Wednesday mornings, as regular as clockwork, they were out on Highway 70 with ten to fifteen million dollars riding in the back.

On Wednesdays, Sawyer had an extra cup of coffee in the barn before they hit the road. It kept him sharp, ready for anything—although, in truth, nothing had ever happened on a Wednesday run, or any other time.

He had been lucky driving Truck 13. DeLuca was a decent partner, if somewhat opinionated. Sawyer had seniority with four years longer on the job, and both of them had Nelson ranked. He was the baby of the family, all six feet seven inches of him, with a pair of hands that made the M-16 they kept in back look like a toy.

Not that they'd ever had to use the rifle, or the shotgun mounted on the dashboard, or the pistols on their hips. Sawyer had never fired a shot himself, except in practice, and he hoped he never would.

Still, you could never tell.

"You hear about that orange alert on the news this morning?" he asked DeLuca.

"Sports arenas, what they said on Channel 7. *Maybe* sports arenas, *maybe* on the coast. Of course, they couldn't say *which* coast. 'No further details. Sorry. As you were.'"

"I hear you."

Ever since the 9/11 attacks, Ohio Armored's management had tried to keep up with the terrorist alerts from Washington, but who could follow all of that? It had been years of running through the color code with "credible" alerts from "trusted" sources, and they never came to anything. Lately, Sawyer suspected the alarms were issued automatically, either to justify the Homeland Security payroll or to make the Feds seem like they were achieving something with their sound and fury.

Mostly, Sawyer thought it was a waste of time and energy, but if he dropped his guard and something happened for a change, it would be his ass in a sling. He was the senior man on Truck 13, and thus responsible for anything that went awry.

He glanced at the odometer and told DeLuca, "We just hit the point of no return."

It was another ritual. DeLuca grunted, as he always did, acknowledging that they would have to top off the gas tank before they started back to Dayton from the capital. The armored truck burned fuel like there was no tomorrow, no price gouging at the pumps, no crisis in the Middle East. Come rain or shine, Truck 13 guzzled gas, and Sawyer didn't want to be caught short when they were on the open road.

Not that a chase was anything to fret about. If anything went down, they had a cell phone and a two-way radio with which to summon reinforcements. State police could reach them any-where along the route within ten minutes, give or take.

Ten minutes wasn't bad.

"We got some company," DeLuca said.

The road ahead was empty, but a square gray van was gaining on them from behind, growing in Sawyer's left-hand mirror. "Let 'em pass, if they're in such a— What the hell? You see that, Joe?"

"See what?" DeLuca asked.

The mirror needed cleaning, which prevented him from see-ing details, but it seemed to Sawyer that a portion of the van's windshield had *opened*. Was that even possible with modern vehicles? Some of the old jeeps used to have windshields that—

"Jesus!"

A jet of flame shot from the dark hole in the van's wind-shield, and Sawyer heard the ringing impact as a high-powered projectile slammed into the rear of his truck. Before his tongue could wrap around the first of the emergency commands they had rehearsed a hundred times, Tom Nelson started screaming in the cargo vault.

DeLuca swiveled in his seat, shouting, "Tommy! What's going on, man?" When the only answer was another high-pitched scream, DeLuca slammed his palm against the speaker. "Listen, dammit! Will you—"

"Joe!" Sawyer shouted. "Wait! He isn't on the intercom."

DeLuca blinked at that, then opened the sliding hatch that screened their only interior view of the vault. He stared at the square of inch-thick glass and then recoiled, gagging.

Sawyer was losing it. So many years of training, practice runs, and still the real thing took him by surprise. His eyes were torn between the road ahead, the gray van in the mirror, and his partner's stricken face. He clutched the steering wheel in hands that ached, their knuckles blanched bone-white.

"What is it, Joe?"

"He's burning," DeLuca moaned. "God Almighty, Tommy's burning up!"

Sawyer could smell it, the scorched-flesh smell he'd never quite forgotten from the summer twelve years earlier, when he had driven past a five-car pileup on the interstate, southeast of Cleveland. Bodies cooking, doused in gasoline.

This smell was different, though.

No gasoline, for one thing—and those corpses hadn't screamed.

"Pull over, Eddie! Jesus!"

"Are you kiddin' me? We're under fire!" he told DeLuca.

"Shit!" DeLuca keyed the intercom and leaned into the speaker, kissing-close, to shout, "Use the extinguisher, Tommy! It's right behind you!"

There were thrashing sounds followed by more screams.

"Get on the radio!" Sawyer snapped. "Get some help out here, right now!"

"The radio. I hear ya."

As DeLuca swung toward the dashboard, reaching out for the microphone, Truck 13 took another hit and began to fishtail. Sawyer fought the swerve, turning a deaf ear to the screams of agony behind him, but he couldn't keep it on the road. Another second passed and he felt the front tires spitting gravel, losing traction. The armored truck rolled over on the driver's side.

1

Clay County, Arkansas

Mack Bolan crouched in darkness, studying the "holy city" from a hundred yards outside its southeastern perimeter. He'd never seen a piece of Paradise on Earth before, but on the rare occasions when he pictured it, his vision had excluded razor wire and guards in camouflage fatigues, with military rifles slung across their shoulders.

Then again, Camp Yahweh wasn't what most mainstream pastors would've called a theological retreat. Its population— 269 at last report—was committed to a militant version of Christian Identity, the "seedline" doctrine that proclaimed Nordic folk the true offspring of Adam, while nonwhite "mud people" sprang from Eve's adulterous affair with Lucifer in reptile form.

Camp Yahweh was a monument to racial hatred, but that didn't make it anything unique in the United States, or in the world at large. There were at least a hundred similar communities that Bolan was aware of, from Alaska to the bayou country of Louisiana, high in the Sierra Madre or—like this one—tucked away in the Ozarks.

Venomous hatred didn't make Camp Yahweh special.

The Executioner was in search of something else.

The eight-foot cyclone fence with razor wire on top was not electrified. He'd tested it on his first visit to the compound, after snapping photos of the layout to prepare himself for penetration. Bolan guessed they'd found the cost of generator fuel prohibitive in recessionary times, when even zealots had to pinch a penny and donations on the neo-Nazi fringe fell short.

He had the compound's blueprint firmly fixed in mind, knew the routines of the soldiers on perimeter patrol and when they were relieved. He didn't know exactly where the object of his search might be concealed, but there were only three apparent possibilities. One unit plainly served as storage. The sentries drew their weapons from another, prior to going on patrol. His third choice was the base command post, occupied by a bearded, long-haired character who could've been auditioning for a part as a nineteenth century mountain man.

Bolan rated the command post unlikely, but he couldn't say for sure until he had a look inside. If he struck out on targets A and B, he'd have to try his luck with C.

But first, he had to get inside.

Bolan crept forward, boots and elbows digging at the soft soil underneath him. He was dressed in black, his face and hands painted to match. The compound wasn't brightly lit, and while they had floodlights mounted in twin watchtowers, north and south, they weren't illuminated at the moment. Bolan guessed that they would save the major candlepower for emergencies or combat drills.

Stay dark, he mentally ordered the sentries in the towers. Don't look down.

Bolan was ready if they saw him, with a Colt Commando assault rifle slung across his back, a .44 Magnum Desert Eagle semiauto pistol on his hip and a sound-suppressing Beretta 93-R selective-fire side arm nestled in a quick-draw armpit rig. His other battle gear included extra magazines for his three firearms, a stiletto, a garrote, grenades and wire cutters.

He used the cutters first, selecting a well-shadowed portion of fence where wild grass had grown taller than usual, nearly knee high. He settled amidst it, waited for the sector guard to pass, then busied himself with the wire. Nocturnal insects covered the sounds that his cutters produced, snipping links on a line two feet high, then six inches across.

Bolan timed his move, slid through the flap, then sealed it loosely behind him with a black twist tie. It wouldn't pass a close inspection, but the guards he had observed so far were young—for Nazis, anyway—and seemed to have no fear of imminent attack.

Indeed, as Bolan knew, there'd been no challenge to their compound at its present site. The first Camp Yahweh, in Missouri, had been raided by a flying squad of FBI and ATF agents in 1997, but the raiders were embarrassed by their failure to discover fugitives or outlawed weapons. The sect had called a press conference to crow about its "victory," then pulled up stakes and moved to Arkansas.

There had been other changes, too. The former Seed of Yahweh was under new management these days, renamed the Aryan Resistance Movement. Its leaders were more militant, more outraged by the slow drift of society toward equal rights for all.

And if the information out of Washington was accurate, they had a deadly secret.

Finding it, defusing it, was Bolan's job.

He lay in shadow, clutching the Beretta, while yet another sentry passed by, heedless of his presence in the weeds. When it was clear, the soldier rose and bolted toward the compound's armory.

He reached it, tried the door and found it locked. Bolan was kneeling, pick in hand, ready to remedy that problem when a scuffling footstep sounded close behind him and a gruff male voice demanded, "Who the fuck are you?"

SIMON GRUNDY LOVED his life. It was a strange thing for him to imagine, knowing where he'd come from—foster homes and juvey hall, a half-assed motorcycle gang, state prison—but it was God's honest truth.

Praise Yahweh.

Who'd have guessed that a habitual offender, malcontent and full-time badass would mature into an officer and gentleman, committed to salvation of his race and nation from encroachment by an enemy who made the Russians and the Red Chinese seem penny-ante by comparison?

Grundy supposed it would've made his mother proud, if she had crawled out of a bottle long enough to focus on her only son for ten or fifteen seconds in her worthless life. As for his father, well, Grundy would need a name to find that shiftless bastard, and it wasn't worth the trouble after thirty-seven years.

The Aryan Resistance Movement was his family now, and that made Grundy proud.

He stood before the mirror in his quarters, counting brushstrokes as he groomed his flowing beard. Most of his troops preferred the skinhead look, but Grundy favored a more biblical style. It could've looked bizarre, but he believed his hulking build and forceful personality made him imposing, rather than ridiculous.

Grundy was midway through stroke ninety-five, just after midnight, when somebody gave a shout outside. He didn't recognize the voice, heard no coherent words, but any breach of Camp Yahweh's decorum was his ultimate responsibility. Grundy set down his brush, considered putting on a shirt, then stepped outside bare-chested.

Let the ladies look, if they were so inclined.

At first glance, from the doorway of his quarters, nothing seemed to be amiss. He checked the towers, then the fence, and found his sentries standing ready, trying to pinpoint the sound. They were having no luck, so far.

The voice had been a man's, but Grundy couldn't say if it had sounded angry, startled or afraid. He ruled out joy, since none of Camp Yahweh's inhabitants would draw attention to themselves with shouts of glee at midnight.

He should count the guards, Grundy decided, make sure none of them had suffered any kind of mishap or—

The fireball nearly blinded him. Its shock wave struck a second later, driving spikes of pain into his eardrums. Grundy rocked back on his heels, with the concussion of the blast, then felt its heat wash over him.

The armory.

He didn't have to guess. Even if Grundy hadn't known Camp Yahweh's layout perfectly, he would've recognized the sound of ammo cooking off, the rapid fire of boxed rounds burning. He instinctively recoiled, crouching, and scuttled back inside his quarters.

What in hell was happening?

He plucked an AR-15 from a wall rack mounted near the door and peered outside again. Guards kept their distance from the flaming ruin of the armory, ducking and dodging slugs that whined through darkness from the pyre. Grundy was on the verge of self-congratulation for their discipline—no panic firing yet—when suddenly an automatic weapon stuttered in the night, some thirty yards east of the burning building.

Full-auto? Something was very wrong.

Machine guns were forbidden in Camp Yahweh. Grundy knew each weapon in the armory—whatever might be left of it—and he examined every private piece brought into camp, from knives to long guns. Nothing was allowed that might provoke another raid, be it a switchblade or a silencer. Up front, at least, he played it strictly by the book.

Which meant that any shooter with full-auto capability was an intruder, wreaking havoc with his men.

Grundy was looking for the prowler's muzzle-flash, tracking his noise, when someone called out in the night, "That isn't one of us!"

The sentries started to converge, drifting off-station from the fence, but Grundy didn't want them moving yet. If there was one intruder in the compound, why not more?

He shouted to the guards, identified himself and ordered them to stand their ground. They were conditioned to obey and did as they were told, although reluctantly. Grundy supposed he'd lose them soon, unless—

"Give me the lights!" he bellowed at the tower guards. "Light up the east side, now!"

As if in answer to his order, yet another thunderous explosion rocked the camp. It was the storage shed this time, roof lifting on a jet of fire that made him think of a volcano spewing lava toward the sky. Two of its walls fell outward, burning, while the others stood in stark relief against the darkness that surrounded them.

Storage.

They kept no arms or ammunition in that shed, but there was fuel for vehicles and generators, propane tanks for cooking. All together, burning fiercely now to light the darkest corners of the camp.

The floodlights blazed, sweeping the compound, bright beams crossing, passing on, returning to the site of the explosion. As they swept across the landscape, Grundy saw a black-clad figure ducking for the shadows, painted face averted from the light.

"Intruder!" he called out to anyone within earshot. Pointing, he ran after the stranger, shouting orders all the way. "Fall in, goddammit! Head him off! I want that prick alive!"

THE EXECUTIONER squeezed off a short burst from his autocarbine as the troops converged. One of his targets stumbled, fell and didn't rise again.

The lights were trouble, tracking him across the compound when he might've otherwise eluded hunters in the dark. Ducking behind a hut that sprouted radio antennas from its angled roof, he craned around the corner, found his mark and milked a 5 or 6 round burst from his stuttergun. The nearest of the floodlights imploded and went dark as soldiers scattered from it, ducking out of sight below the tower's waist-high walls.

Someone—perhaps the mountain man—was shouting orders at the other troops, coordinating the advance. They hadn't cornered Bolan yet, but it could happen, if he didn't stay ahead of them. Step one was blacking out the other light before it marked his place and someone on the sidelines made a lucky shot.

He saw the glaring beam wash over his position, even though it couldn't find him in the shadow of the small communications hut. It wouldn't take the sentries long to close around him, pin him down, and numbers could defeat him then. He wasn't Superman, wasn't invincible. A storm of fire would drop him where he stood, like anybody else, unless he found a way out of the trap.

Lights first.

Taking a chance, he stepped into the open, raised his weapon, sighting down the beam of that all-seeing eye. Before the startled hunters could react, Bolan triggered another burst and blacked out the floodlight, toppling one of its minders from his lofty perch into a screaming swan dive to the earth below.

The sudden darkness covered him, but not for long. On orders from their chief, the camp's guards were advancing, still maintaining discipline of fire, but it would only take one glimpse of Bolan in the shadows, one stray shot, to spark chaos.

Why wait?

Bolan fired two quick rounds toward the west, then pivoted, already moving, and triggered two more to the east. He was running south toward the command post when someone to the east returned his fire, immediately echoed by a weapon to the west.

Good hunting, Bolan thought, and left them to it. Gunfire popped and crackled through the compound, drowning out the gruff voice of the officer who tried to shout it down. The leader would have a rough time with control, Bolan calculated, but the danger hadn't passed, by any means. A stray shot could be just as deadly as a sniper's well-aimed bullet, and the sudden crash in discipline meant sentries would be trigger-happy all around the compound.

Bolan concentrated on his first task, pushing on through firelight and shadows toward the command post. If the object he sought wasn't there, he was stumped—and that boded ill for his mission.

Where *was* it?

What was it?

Bolan had hoped he'd recognize the object when he saw it, but so far the camp had yielded nothing even close to what he sought. If he struck out at the CP, he'd have to seek another source of inside information that could put him on the track.

Inside.

Someone from Camp Yahweh might do the trick, but that would mean escaping with a hostage under fire. It would be risky, at the very least, perhaps impossible. A last resort, in any case.

Bolan stayed focused on his first priority. The camp CP was fifty yards in front of him, with two men posted on the porch. He saw no trace of the leader, guessing that the bearded officer would be among his troops.

So much the better.

Closing from their right-hand side, the Executioner drew the 93-R from its armpit rig and triggered two quick shots. The nearer guard collapsed as if he were a puppet and someone had snipped his strings. The other spun to face a danger he couldn't identify, and Bolan dropped him with a quiet Parabellum round between the eyes.

He left them there, shrouded in shadows, and passed through an unlocked door into the boss man's private quarters. They were neat enough, but still possessed a kind of musky odor that he couldn't place.

Ignore it, he thought.

Bolan swiftly checked any hiding places he could think of in the Spartan quarters: closets, footlocker, beneath the sturdy cot. He checked desk drawers, in hope of finding sketches, plans, perhaps a note that would direct him to a secret cache.

Nothing.

Bolan retraced his steps through empty rooms, back to the porch. The two dead guards were lying where he'd left them, but they weren't alone.

Five gunmen ringed the porch, all watching Bolan over weapons pointed at his chest.

"DROP THE WEAPON! Raise your hands! Don't move!"

The shouted orders echoed from behind Simon Grundy, causing him to turn and squint through firelight toward his quarters. Several of his men were clustered there, pointing their weapons at a tall man on the porch.

A tall man dressed in black, faces and hands painted with combat cosmetics to match.

"Hold up, there!" Grundy shouted at them. "Don't—"

Before he could complete the thought, a burst of automatic fire blazed from the stranger's weapon, toppling one of Grundy's troopers from the porch. At the same instant, as if propelled by his weapon's recoil, the trespasser sprang backward, slammed the door with his free hand and disappeared.

The others started pouring fire into the bungalow, as fast as they could pull the triggers on their AR-15 carbines. Bullets drilled the wall, blew out the windows, rattled the vibrating door in its frame. Grundy imagined his belongings in there, shot to hell, but he was focused on the stranger.

"Cease-fire, dammit!" Rushing among them, he grabbed first one rifleman and then another, wrestling them off target, shouting in their faces to be heard above the small-arms racket. "Hold your fire! I want that bastard breathing!"

"Too late, Major," one of them replied. The youngster grinned and giggled.

"Oh, you think so?" Grundy shoved him toward the bullet-scarred front door. "So, get in there and check it out."

The skinhead hesitated, then put on his war face, nodded once and rushed the door. He didn't think to try the knob, but kicked it open, Grundy waving others in behind him as he rushed the living room.

There was no body in the living room, no blood to indicate that any of his men had scored a hit with their wild firing through the wall and windows. They fanned out, checking the corners, even though they offered no concealment for a man-sized target.

Stalling.

Grundy led them to the bedroom door, which he knew he had left ajar. The trespasser had closed it, and two bullet holes marked the painted surface, as if peepholes had been carelessly installed, off center and at different levels.

"Nowhere else for him to go," one of the soldiers said. They moved in closer, ringed the door with scowls and steel.

Grundy was trembling, but he couldn't order one of them to go ahead of him this time. What would they think, if he sent someone else to check his sleeping quarters, maybe check under the bed for bogeymen.

Clutching his piece one-handed, Grundy turned the knob and shoved the door back with sufficient force to make it strike the wall, crouching as it swung open. Reinforcements crowded close behind him, leaning in to aim above his head and shoulders. If they fired, he would be deafened, but he didn't mind the company just then.

The empty room made nonsense of their melodrama. Grundy rushed the closet, threw it open to reveal his extra uniforms, but no intruder hiding there. As he turned back to face the room, two of his men were peering underneath the cot from different sides and making faces at each other.

"Nothing," one of them declared.

"The window's unlocked, Major."

Grundy saw it closed, the way he'd left it, but the corporal was right. The latch was open now. He always kept it locked from force of habit. Someone else had opened it, used it as an escape hatch. Leaning closer, he saw scuff marks on the wall, probably from boots.

"Outside!" he shouted. "Make a sweep! We have to find out where he went and stop him. If he gets away…"

He meant to say, *We'll never know who sent him*, but his soldiers were already rushing out, not waiting for the why and wherefore of it. Orders were enough for them, these fine young savages. They lived for action, didn't give a damn why they were fighting, as long as someone tagged the mission with a rousing call for race and honor.

They were children, but they weren't afraid of dirty work.

He followed them outside, eyes sweeping Camp Yahweh for any sign of the intruder or companions who had thus far managed to avoid detection. Were there others, lurking in the shadows? Were they Feds or mercenaries? Members of some rival nationalist movement or some leftist private army?

There was only one way to find out.

He had to capture one alive and make him squeal.

"Stay sharp!" he ordered his assembled soldiers. "Cover every corner of the camp. We need—"

Across the compound, at the motor pool, an engine growled and headlights blazed. Before Grundy could snap out a fresh command, one of their jeeps was off and racing toward the gate.

THE JEEP was military surplus, which required no key. Bolan needed a ram to breach the gate, and speed to give him an advantage on Camp Yahweh's infantry. A mile would do it, if he got that far. He could discard the stolen wheels, then, and proceed on foot to reach his own.

But first, he had to make it out of camp alive.

About the time that his pursuers finished ransacking the CP hut, he slid into the driver's seat, reviewed the world's simplest controls and gunned the jeep to life. There was no point in running dark, since they could see him by the light of leaping flames in any case, so Bolan used the high beams as offensive weapons, blinding any troops who stood directly in his path.

There weren't that many of them. Most had rushed to join their CO at his quarters, or else fanned out to police the camp's perimeter. Of the dependents in Camp Yahweh, the wives and children of the "Master Race" commandos, Bolan had seen nothing yet and hoped to keep it that way. They were not civilians in the strictest sense, having withdrawn from civilized society to live a racist pipe dream fraught with danger, but he didn't want them in his line of fire, if it could be avoided.

Wherever they were hiding, none of them emerged as Bolan made his short run toward the gate. He gunned the jeep to its top speed, aimed at the double gates a hundred yards downrange. Two guards were stationed there, and by the time he'd covered half the distance to his target, others were arriving, racing to assist their comrades.

Others still were firing from behind him, peppering the jeep with semiauto fire that struck like ringing hammer blows. A hollow *thunk* told Bolan that one round had drilled the gas can mounted on the tailgate, but he knew he had fuel enough to get where he was going, and the gunmen would need tracer rounds to set the sloshing gasoline on fire.

Racing across the open camp, he swerved the jeep from side to side, ducking as low as possible while still maintaining visibility across the dashboard. By the time he'd covered fifty yards, the windshield was a pile of pebbled safety glass in Bolan's lap and strewed around his feet. Sparks flew from glancing bullet strikes, while solid hits drilled through the fenders, flaking paint in perfect circles.

Thirty yards.

The soldiers on the gate were firing at him now, so Bolan aimed his autocarbine through the empty windshield frame and held down the trigger, sweeping its muzzle back and forth in short arcs, left and right. The Colt Commando's 30-round magazine emptied in less than three seconds, but it lasted long enough to sweep the resistance from the gate and scatter bodies in Bolan's path. One thumped beneath the tires before the Jeep hit the chain-link gates and powered through.

Behind him, gunfire stuttered on for several seconds, but Bolan quickly killed the headlights and robbed them of their target. It was open country for another hundred yards or so, before he hit tall grass approaching spotty woods. Beyond that point, he had to risk the low beams as he sought a winding path around and through the trees.

Pursuit was possible, since Bolan hadn't taken time to disable the other vehicles in camp, but it would take some time to organize, and he would see the headlights coming. By the time they found the abandoned jeep, Bolan would've found his way on foot back to the rental car he'd stashed a mile due north of Camp Yahweh.

If any of them followed Bolan that far, it would be their last mistake.

He found a place to park, then changed his mind and pushed the vehicle into a ravine with water rippling somewhere near the bottom. There was no point making its retrieval easy on the enemy, he thought. At that point, leaving empty-handed, any inconvenience he could cause was a victory of sorts.

And Bolan wasn't finished with the Aryan Resistance Movement yet.

Camp Yahweh hadn't yielded what he hoped to find, but there were other places he could look, people he could interrogate.

He wasn't giving up.

The cost of failure was too high, in terms of human lives and suffering.

When Bolan's job was done, the enemy would know it.

Those, that was, who'd managed to survive.

2

Two days earlier

A coded-access steel door barred them from the War Room at Stony Man Farm. Barbara Price keyed in her access code, then crossed the threshold as the heavy door slid open. Mack Bolan followed, heard the door shut behind him as he scanned the conference table for familiar faces.

Hal Brognola sat at the head of the table, flanked by Aaron Kurtzman in a wheelchair on his left, two empty chairs immediately on his right for Price and Bolan. Next to Kurtzman, facing one of the empties, sat Huntington Wethers, an African/American cybernetics specialist who'd been lured to the Farm team from a full professorship at Berkeley.

Bolan nodded all around in lieu of handshakes, took his seat and answered the usual small talk about his flight. Even with the chitchat still in progress, he could see Brognola stewing, anxious to be on about the business that had brought them all together.

"We've been saddled with a problem," Brognola began, as if the team had ever been assembled to receive good news.

"I'm listening," Bolan replied.

"Maybe you heard about the tank incident in Baghdad a few months ago?"

Bolan frowned. "Specifics?"

"An Abrams tank was on routine patrol when it was hit by *something* that burned through the side skirts and armor on one side, grazed the gunner's flack jacket and sliced through the back of his seat, then drilled a pencil-sized hole almost two inches deep into the four-inch armor on the turret's other side. No projectile was recovered. Officially, the incident remains unexplained."

"And unofficially?" Bolan asked.

"The Pentagon's as worried as hell. They don't know what they're dealing with, who's got it, how many are out there—in short, they don't know a damned thing."

"A secret weapon," Bolan said. "Each war produces innovations and surprises. Put the SEALs or Special Forces on it. Shake things up. They'll find a guy who knows a guy and track it down."

"No luck with that so far," Kurtzman said. "Top priority or otherwise, they're pumping dry holes over there."

"One logical alternative," Bolan replied, "is a defective weapon of some kind. Guerrillas mix and match. Sometimes they fabricate to meet their needs. New weapons frequently have unpredictable results when they're first used in combat. Maybe your hotshot was a mistake, and they've worked out the bugs."

"We don't think so," Brognola said.

"Why not?"

"Because it's surfaced in the States."

Bolan leaned forward in his chair. "Say what?"

"On Wednesday morning, in Ohio," the big Fed confirmed. "There's no mistake."

"Go on."

"Somebody hit an armored truck en route from Dayton to Columbus, carrying 65 million dollars. Somebody fired twice through the back doors with the supergun—whatever. Cooked the guard back there and spooked the driver, so he rolled it. After that, they used conventional C-4 to pop the doors, iced the witnesses, then made off with the cash."

"That's all we have?" Bolan asked.

"Not quite," Brognola said. "The guards up front got off a

radio alarm about the hit. An old gray van, they said, and 'something weird,' which pretty much describes the supergun. A couple of state troopers saw the van and started a pursuit."

"I'm guessing that they didn't catch it," Bolan said.

"You're right. The fugitives lit up a gasoline truck, killed the driver, forced the troopers off the highway, set the fields on fire."

"The troopers?" Bolan asked.

"One of them's in a Cincinnati burn ward as we speak. The other didn't make it."

"What about the van?"

"Stolen out of St. Louis two weeks earlier," Brognola said. "Painted and overhauled. They torched it outside Louisville, Kentucky. Wiped out anything forensically significant, but they left stolen license plates from Little Rock, and we could still see how they modified the van inside."

"Is that significant?" Bolan asked.

"Absolutely," Wethers interjected. "First, they built a swivel unit where the backseat used to be, then ditched the shotgun seat and fixed the windshield so the right-hand side would lower on a hinge."

"To fire the supergun," Bolan said.

"In our estimation, yes. With the arrangement we discovered, they could aim it fore or aft. They made it mobile, and it served them well."

"Too bad we don't know who *they* are," Bolan remarked.

"I just might have a lead on that," Brognola said. "It isn't definite, by any means, but—"

"Give me what you have," the Executioner replied.

"How much do you know about Christian Identity?" Brognola asked.

"A neo-Nazi version of King James. The Nordic tribes of Israel. Jews are demons, nonwhites are mud people, the usual racist garbage."

"That's it, in a nutshell," Brognola said, "with the emphasis on nuts. It used to be the creed of choice with white supremacists until the 1990s, when a lot of them turned Odinist to claim their Viking roots. The hard core hanging with Identity is more extreme than ever now, maybe to balance what they lost in numbers."

"If you want to call that balanced," Wethers said.

"In any case," Brognola said, forging ahead, "we've got a clique of suspects who line up with the events in question geographically. Are you familiar with an outfit called the Aryan Resistance Movement?"

"Not offhand," Bolan replied.

"Aaron?"

Kurtzman keyed a button from his chair, and Bolan watched a screen descend behind Brognola. From the far wall opposite, a slide projector hummed to life, projecting a map of the central U.S. on the screen. Brognola half turned in his chair to eye the map, as he continued speaking.

"They're a neo-Nazi outfit, as you might imagine from the name. Still clinging to Identity theology, against the far-right trend. They have a compound here." He pointed to the northeastern corner of Arkansas with an infrared beam. "You'll find their background information in the file I brought you, but to summarize, they started in Missouri, then moved south, and they've been getting more extreme—more militant—as time goes by. Nonsense about the call to topple ZOG, and so on."

"That's the Zionist Occupation Government,'" Barbara Price reminded him. "Otherwise known as the U.S. of A."

Bolan nodded, familiar with the term from other contacts on the fascist fringe. He waited for Brognola to continue.

"Anyway," Brognola said, "geography." The pointer danced across the broad projected map as he continued. "Here we've got the ARM, holed up in what they call Camp Yahweh. A hundred miles to the southwest is Little Rock, source of the stolen license plates. Due north, St. Louis, where the movement got its start—"

"And where the van was stolen," Bolan finished for him.

"Right, you are. Ohio, where they made the hit on Wednesday, is a straight shot, more or less, from northern Arkansas along the interstates. And coming back, there's Louisville. Stop by and torch the van that's served its purpose."

"It's suggestive," Bolan said, "but it's also circumstantial."

"Granted, but we're looking for a weapon, not preparing for a trial."

"Okay," Bolan replied. "Convince me."

"Right. For starters, three known members of the ARM were once associated with the Phineas Priesthood and the Aryan Republican Army."

Both of those groups, Bolan knew, had robbed banks and armored cars across the United States in the 1990s to finance a scheme they liked to call Racial Holy War. Some members had been prosecuted and were serving time, but others wriggled through the nets for want of solid evidence connecting them to a specific crime. Broader sedition charges filed against both groups had been dismissed on grounds that anyone in the U.S. was free to advocate destruction of the government, as long as they made no attempt to pull it off.

"All right, we're closer," Bolan said.

"It's apparent from the new group's publications that they idolize the Phineans and ARA," Brognola added, "but their straight-up heroes are Bob Mathews and The Order."

In the early 1980s The Order—also called the Silent Brotherhood—had blazed a path of mayhem across the Pacific Northwest. Its membership was never more than twenty-five or thirty diehards, but the group had declared war on "Red America" and financed its campaign with a series of daring armed robberies that netted several million dollars from banks and Brinks trucks.

"You're looking for a blueprint," Bolan said.

"Already found it," Brognola replied. "It's right there in *The Turner Diaries.*"

Bolan nodded, frowning. While he hadn't read the novel, self-published in 1978 by a former physics professor turned Nazi guru for a pack of dim-witted disciples, Bolan knew the basic plot: America, enslaved by "ZOG," is rescued from the brink of race-mixing and social chaos by a band of vigilantes called The Order, who rob banks, hang "race traitors" and finally demolish Congress with a huge truck bomb. The *Diaries* had inspired a host of homegrown terrorists over the past quarter century, from Mathews and the real-life Order to various Klansmen, militias and the Oklahoma City bomber.

Playing the devil's advocate, Bolan noted the obvious. "They're not the only bunch of redneck psychopaths who have the *Diaries* memorized. I'm guessing you could point to six or seven other groups right now, within the same half-dozen states."

"You're right again. I could. But only one of them has been in touch with this guy. Aaron?"

On the screen, a grinning face replaced the map. The man was bearded, sunburned, appearing to be an Arab. He looked vaguely familiar to Bolan.

"Wadi Amal bin Sadr," Brognola declared. "He's an Iraqi Shiite cleric, presently in exile. We've had sightings from Tehran to Paris, but the only one confirmed so far was here."

The picture changed again. This time, the man stood with two Caucasian males. Flat desert and a small adobe building could be seen in the background. All of them were smiling for the camera, apparently delighted to be there.

"Wadi again," Brognola said, aiming his pointer at the second face in line. "This one is Curt Walgren, self-styled supreme commander of the ARM, and on his left is Barry James, his second in command."

They didn't look like much to Bolan, though they could've been a pair of Gulf War veterans in their desert camouflage fatigues. Bush hats concealed what might have been evidence of skinhead sympathies, or simply military-style buzz cuts. They had no visible tattoos, and sunglasses concealed their eyes. About all he could judge from the group photo was their strong, white teeth.

"When did they meet?" Bolan asked.

"This was taken in October," Brognola replied, "outside of Ciudad Juarez. That's just across the Tex-Mex border from El Paso."

"Been there," Bolan said.

"Oh, right."

"Stop me if I'm mistaken, now," Bolan began. "Our theory is that Sadr passed the supergun along to these yahoos, so they could—what? Rob armored cars? Raise hell at random in the States?"

"We can't ask Sadr," Brognola answered. "Rumor is the Israelis vaporized him with a rocket attack in Jordan, last week, but I doubt that we'll ever confirm it. Motive-wise, there's not much difference between his sect and what passes for Christianity inside the ARM. They both hate Israel and believe that Jews are children of the devil. Both regard the U.S. government as a Satanic instrument. Walgren would spit on Sadr for the color of his skin, but if the Arab helps him hit the Jews, he'd play along. You know the old saying—'The enemy of my enemy is my friend.'"

Bolan nodded. "It's logical enough," he said. "You think they've got the weapon stashed at their compound in Arkansas?"

"When we connect the dots, that's where they lead."

"No inside information, though?"

The man from Justice shook his head. "So far, the ARM has been impervious to infiltration. Strict security, including polygraphs for all prospective members and alleged initiation ceremonies that would compromise a law-enforcement officer."

"Participation in some criminal activity," Brognola said. "The rumors range from strong-arm robbery to murder."

"No defectors? Rejects who tried out but didn't make the cut?"

"None we're aware of," Price replied. "It makes us...curious."

"Okay," Bolan said, nodding toward the fat manila folder resting on the table. "I'd better read that file."

BROGNOLA HAD FLOWN back to Washington after the briefing, leaving Barbara Price and her team at Stony Man to answer any questions Bolan had after he'd read the dossier on Walgren and the ARM.

Bolan had one question that he wouldn't have asked Brognola, in any case. "What do you really think about this mission, Barb?"

She frowned and told him, "Everybody from the Pentagon to Pennsylvania Avenue has been looking for this supergun. It wasn't high priority while they were looking in Baghdad, but now someone has brought the war home to the States. Right now, the ARM is what we've got, in terms of leads. It's *something*, and we need to run it down."

"I see the group's suspected in a string of cases, going back to its foundation, in Missouri."

"Right." She nodded. "Stickups in the early days. Some bombings—an abortion clinic, gay bars, a Missouri synagogue. Some deaths and disappearances. No charges ever stuck."

In fact, as Bolan knew, few charges had been filed. Two members of the ARM had been indicted for the synagogue attack, but jurors had acquitted them after a witness changed her testimony. Several deaths and disappearances had been connected to the group—including the peculiar "suicide" of Walgren's predecessor, hanged with hands duct-taped behind his back—but no indictments had been filed.

"Could be a hornet's nest," he said, "or a wild-goose chase."

"You don't like to waste the time."

"It's not a waste if it pays off. But I'd feel better if we had a pair of eyes inside."

"The Bureau tried, back in the day," she said.

He'd seen that in the file. One of the missing persons theoretically connected to the ARM had been an FBI informant who dropped out of sight soon after he applied for membership.

Headquarters still suspected Walgren's people had disposed of him, but they had never found the body, and their spy had also irritated heavy hitters from at least two other far-right paramilitary groups along the way. His death could be attributed to any of those enemies.

No evidence, no case.

"I guess there's only one way to find out," the warrior said at last.

"When are you heading out?" she asked.

"First thing tomorrow. Have a look around the place tomorrow night, then pop in for a visit the day after."

"What's Plan B, if you don't find the supergun?"

"I've got some names and addresses," Bolan said. "If I can't grab someone from the compound for a chat, I'll work my way around the circuit. It's a small world, on the fringe."

"Still easy to get lost in," Price said.

"I'll light a candle," Bolan told her. "Maybe leave a trail of bread crumbs."

"Just so you come back."

"That's always in the plan."

She didn't tell him what they both already knew, that best-laid plans often went sour during life-or-death engagements with the enemy. She didn't have to say it, since that message was tattooed on Bolan's soul, and on her own.

"Tomorrow early, then," she said.

"The proverbial crack of dawn. I've got a flight out of Fort Pickett at seven o'clock, to Camp Robinson outside North Little Rock."

"You need your rest, then."

Bolan shrugged. "I don't mind sleeping in the air."

"I think you ought to be in bed."

His smile was cautious. "Do you want to go upstairs?"

"I thought you'd never ask."

3

Bolan's secondary target lay across the Arkansas-Missouri line, some thirty miles away, at Poplar Bluff. The man he wanted was a gunsmith for the ARM, one Neville Alan Hoskins. Friends called him "Chopper," in homage to his fondness for machine guns, but rumors persisted that certain jailhouse wolves had dubbed him "Nellie" when he pulled a five-spot in Atlanta, for weapons and explosives violations.

Federal dossiers named Hoskins as an ARM member who stayed "in the world," conducting business of a sort in mainstream society while serving the cause when he could. Rumor had it that his services included the purchase of banned weapons and conversion of semiautomatic civilian arms to full-auto illegals, but no such charges had been proved since his emergence from the pen.

From all outward appearances, Hoskins and his small appliance repair shop in Poplar Bluff were completely legitimate, if decidedly low-rent and on the terminally scruffy side. The photos Bolan had examined didn't show a classic member of the Master Race, by any means.

He hadn't taken out the commo hut at Camp Yahweh, but he'd done the next best thing—alerting county sheriff's officers to the attack while he was on the run—assuring that the compound would be overrun with uniforms before another hour passed. Still, Bolan knew his adversaries could've spread the word on his attack before he'd reached the county line. And while that posed no threat to him per se, he feared that those he hunted might escape to parts unknown if they were spooked.

It all depended on the system of communication from Camp Yahweh. First alerts would go to those who ran the ARM—Curt Walgren, Barry James and their top aides. Beyond that, if they had no network for emergency alerts in place, the news might spread haphazardly, skip certain members altogether. Then again, they might turn on their TV sets and catch the live broadcast of the search for bodies at Camp Yahweh on all the news channels.

There was a chance that Neville Hoskins wasn't in the loop, so far, and that the neo-Nazi armorer might have at least some clue about the nature and whereabouts of a certain mystery weapon. If Bolan could find him, the gunsmith would spill what he knew. That much was guaranteed.

If Bolan could find him.

The Executioner reached Poplar Bluff without incident, no sign of patrol cars on the highway or the city streets. It seemed to be a dead night in the Show Me State, and Bolan hoped that it would stay that way. His mission in the town of eighteen thousand could be a relatively simple one—or it could go to hell in nothing flat, if things went wrong.

He found the combination shop and residence where Hoskins hung his overalls, circling the block to check for lookouts on the street. In light of what had happened farther south, Bolan supposed police might have the place staked out, or soldiers from the ARM might've rallied to a brother who had served them well. If there were any watchers on the quiet street, though, they were well concealed.

He made a second pass, then parked his rental car two doors north of Ace Appliance and cut through a silent yard to reach the alleyway in back. Jeans and a nylon windbreaker covered Bolan's blacksuit, while his hands and face were stripped of war paint. He could pass a casual inspection in the seedy neighborhood, as long as no one checked beneath his jacket, where the sleek, silent Beretta nestled in its shoulder rig.

Against all odds, the gunsmith had no dogs. Bolan had been concerned that he might have to deal with Dobermans or pit bulls in the yard, but no such threat materialized. Instead, he simply had to hop a sagging chain-link fence and sneak up on his target's dark apartment from the rear.

So far, so good.

The back porch sagged and groaned under his weight, two-hundred-plus pounds added to the appliances and parts collected there with no apparent system to their storage. Bolan tried the back door, certain that it would be locked, and froze when it moved at his touch.

Was it a trap, or was his quarry simply careless? Bolan drew his Beretta, stepping well back from the doorway as he gave the door a shove. It swung wide open on a kitchen redolent of grease and deep-fried food. No guns blazed, no burglar alarms shrieked for attention in the predawn silence. After another cautious moment, probing with his mind and senses, the soldier stepped across the threshold into the unknown.

The kitchen was a long-established mess. Whatever else Hoskins believed in, sound nutrition hadn't made the list. For all its grime and clutter, though, the room held no proof that its owner had evacuated. Neither did the living room, where empty beer cans had assumed the status of an art form, posed on every flat surface available. The kitchen's oil smell gave way, in this room, to stale sweat and mildew.

Bolan found the proof of hasty exit in his target's bedroom. There, general disorder of his living space gave way to ransacked chaos. Drawers from a cheap dresser had been dumped out and discarded. Wire hangers from the closet made a trail across the floor, some of them bent where clothing had been jerked away. Presumably, the missing items had been packed, since Hoskins's bedroom had less clutter on the floor than any other room Bolan had seen, so far.

There had been weapons in the closet, too. He could smell the oil and solvent. His guns were probably the only thing Hoskins had truly cared for, beer aside, and they were gone. Besides the lingering aroma, all Hoskins had missed was a half box of .357 Magnum cartridges, pushed back into a corner on the topmost closet shelf.

Something had spooked the Nazi gunsmith. Whether it was Bolan's raid in Arkansas or something else, the end result was still identical.

Hoskins was gone, without a forwarding address.

And Bolan had to choose another target from his shrinking list.

"So, WHAT'S THE FINAL body count?" Curt Walgren asked.

"Holding at nine dead, seven wounded," Barry James replied. "Grundy's ass-deep in cops and Feds."

"Of course he is. They'll tear the place apart before they're finished. Where's our fucking lawyer?"

"On his way," James answered in a soothing tone. "I had to wake him up."

"The rates we pay, I don't care if you had to raise him from the dead. I want him shadowing those cops and Feds. Make sure they don't take anything that isn't specified by warrant."

"He knows what to do."

"He'd better." Walgren bolted down his second shot of straight tequila, left the glass and went to sit directly opposite his chief lieutenant. "All right, Barry, what the hell is this about?"

"You have to ask?"

"Ohio? That's impossible."

"Is it?"

"The Feds suspect us, naturally. They would be total morons if they didn't," Walgren said. "But they need *evidence*. They come with warrants, not like this. Some joker with a painted face, running around at midnight, blowing things to hell. Give me a break."

"Black ops, remember? Christ, we've talked enough about it from day one."

"They pull that shit in other countries, Barry. Black ops in the States means bugs and wiretaps, stings, entrapment, setting up an ambush when they have the chance."

"All right," James said. "Who else is there?"

Walgren echoed his aide's own words. "You have to ask? Think Yiddish. Try Mossad, maybe the JDL."

James thought about it for a moment. "I don't think so, Curt."

"Why not?"

"Mossad might bomb your car or shoot you on the street, but this is too high profile for an operation in the States. Also, they'd never send a single man to pull a deal like this. Same thing for Jewish Defense League, assuming they had any talent on this scale."

"So, it's a mystery? We let it go at that?"

"Nobody's saying let it go. We just have to be careful now, with so much going on. The last thing we need, with the big day so close, is some kind of high-profile vendetta," James said in caution.

"Play it cool, you're saying."

"Right."

"Roll with the punch."

"Until we know who threw it, anyway."

"And then?"

James shrugged. "We choose the time and place for payback. Make it count."

"You always were conservative," Walgren said.

"That's why I get the big bucks, right?"

Walgren could only smile at that. "We'll think about it, Barry. In the meantime, get that shyster on the line, will you? Make sure he's earning every goddamned cent we pay him."

"Right. Will do." James rose and stiffened to attention, clicked his heels and snapped off a straight-arm salute. "Hail victory!"

Walgren responded from his chair, halfheartedly. When James was gone, he rose and crossed the room, pushed through another door into his private sleeping chamber. There he sat, relaxed as best he could, as he addressed his mirror image.

"So, you heard all that?"

"I always hear," his reflection said.

"Barry wants to cool it. See what happens."

"What do we want?"

"Waiting sucks," Walgren said. "It's cowardly. It sends the wrong message."

"Make an example, then."

"Of who?"

"It's *whom*."

"All right. Of *whom?*"

"Identity is less important than impact," the mirror image answered. "In a totally corrupt society, who are the innocents?"

"No one."

"Precisely. All except the faithful are complicit in the crime."

"All guilty should be punished," Walgren said.

"In time. Until that day…"

"A choice."

"*Our* choice."

"A demonstration."

"An example."

"Good."

The choice would be a challenge, with so many enemies around them. Still, Curt Walgren knew whatever choice he made would be the proper one. He was inspired, at times like these, with a perception and intelligence beyond his normal limits.

In such moments, he knew how the old-time prophets felt, spreading the word of Yahweh to a world that didn't care and wouldn't listen. A reckoning would follow, and the unbelievers would be punished for their doubts, their mockery. Walgren would supervise their punishment himself, and he would glory in it.

But until that day…

There was a demonstration to arrange, and he had to also

make concerted efforts to identify the enemy responsible for the attack upon Camp Yahweh.

It was not a crippling blow, would not defeat them or postpone the great day that was coming, but it still required an answer. James was wrong about the wait-and-see approach, which only signaled weakness to an enemy and thus encouraged him to strike again. Retaliation was the answer, and a larger demonstration to society at large.

A warning of the wrath that was to come.

One man against a small army.

Who had such skill and daring? Walgren wondered. His worst enemies were Jews, the schemers after world dominion, but it seemed incredible to him that the U.S. could produce such fighters. Israel had been forced to breed them, train them from the cradle upward, but Americans were soft by definition, their pampered minorities all the more so. They lacked discipline, determination, and the will to sacrifice.

The man who had rampaged through Camp Yahweh might be an Aryan, given the courage and ability he had displayed. Who *was* he? Why had he chosen this, of all times, to attack the Aryan Resistance Movement?

James was right. It had to be Ohio.

Dammit!

"Never mind," his mirror image said. As always, the reflected face could read his thoughts, almost before they formed inside his head. "We'll make it right."

"We have to," Walgren echoed.

"And we will."

"Identify the enemy."

"Identify and locate."

"Locate and destroy."

"In Yahweh's name."

"*Amen!*"

4

Bolan drove through the night and predawn hours to reach his next target in Russellville, Missouri, a few miles southwest of Jefferson City. It was the last target Bolan could reach that day, without a plane ride, and he hoped to make it count.

The man he wanted, Vernon Upshaw, was a former high school English social studies teacher, driven from his job when he began insinuating Nazi propaganda into daily lesson plans. Around the time he told a class of freshmen that the Holocaust was a colossal hoax created in the postwar years by Communists and the "Jews Media," the school board cut him loose and his appeals had been rejected by the courts. Since then, Upshaw had turned his questionable talents to production of the Aryan Resistance Movement's monthly newsletter and sundry other publications, printed in the basement of a house that he'd inherited from relatives.

Bolan had the address, and dawn seemed like a good time for a pop quiz with the former teacher. If he passed, and didn't raise a fuss, maybe Upshaw would live to foul another day.

Maybe.

The house was small, situated in a neighborhood that had outlived its glory days. The people Bolan saw leaving for early shifts at work were mostly Hispanic or black, a circumstance that had to have rankled Upshaw. He was caught in the classic bigot's dilemma: live with nonwhite neighbors, or risk selling his Aryan homestead to more of the same. It was the kind of problem that would keep a Nazi up at night.

Bolan was ready with a wake-up call.

He parked in front, walked up and rang the bell. He sensed neighbors were watching as he waited on the tiny porch. There was no answer from within, leaving Bolan to choose a point of entry in broad daylight, under scrutiny.

With nothing much to lose, he tried the front door's knob and felt it turn. A chilly sense of déjà vu washed over Bolan as he slid a hand inside his windbreaker, gripping the pistol in its armpit rig, and brainstormed on the call.

He couldn't go all SWAT-team on the threshold, with the local busybodies studying his every move. Likewise, if Bolan left the stoop and went around back, suspicious neighbors might alert police. He couldn't count on them dismissing it as "white man's business," where their homes and families were concerned. Potential crimes in progress were a danger to the neighborhood at large, and Bolan thought someone was sure to phone it in.

Which left a classic bluff.

Watchers could see him, but they probably couldn't hear him, unless they were shadowing the house with advanced electronic surveillance equipment. It was also unlikely that they could see past him and into Upshaw's living room if he opened the door. For all they knew, their racist neighbor could be welcoming an early-morning visitor.

Of course, the bluff would put Bolan's life at risk. He couldn't draw his weapon or take any other normal duck-and-cover steps to guard himself against an ambush or a booby trap. He'd had to mime a conversation, step inside as if by Upshaw's invitation and proceed to search the place after he'd closed the door.

And if Upshaw was waiting for him, with a weapon pointed at the door, Bolan would know it in the split-second before he died.

He gave the door a shove, quickly withdrew his hand and raised it in a gesture of greeting. No muzzle-flash erupted from the inner darkness, and he heard no clamoring alarms, but that still didn't mean the house was empty, much less safe.

Bolan went through the motions, mouthing silent words although he wasn't sure that any watchers had a clear view of his lips. He nodded once, then shrugged, nodded again, and stepped across the threshold into Upshaw's murky living room. He used a heel to shut the door behind him, cutting off the light.

The drapes were drawn, which would shut out the neighbors, but also left him in a twilight world of hulking shadows. Bolan found a wall switch, flicked it, and a pair of tall, cheap-looking lamps provided ample light to see that no one else was in the room. He drew the pistol, took a chance and called out Upshaw's name. His voice fell flat and dead within the musty silence of the house.

Nobody home? Nobody answering, for sure.

He made a rapid tour of the kitchen, bathroom, two small bedrooms and the basement. There was no one to be found, and while Upshaw's abode was tidier than that of Neville Hoskins, it revealed signs of a swift and unexpected exit. Coffee had been brewing when the tenant left, but it had long gone cold. Dust patterns on a bedroom dresser told him that a six-by-ten-inch box was missing, likely Upshaw's nest egg or a jewelry box. The only evidence of weapons was a small oil stain on one of Upshaw's pillows.

As for any superguns, no dice.

In the basement propaganda mill, Bolan sifted through stacks of newsletters and pamphlets with a common theme: Jews were the spawn of Satan, blamed for ninety-odd percent of all recorded wars and natural disasters from Old Testament times to the present. Upshaw strung events together, from famines to assassinations to volcanic eruptions, in a panorama of conspiracy that would've been hilarious—if some sick minds didn't regard it as the gospel truth.

One pamphlet, undated but bundled and ready for shipping,

was headlined: *THE DAY IS AT HAND!!!* Below a crude sketch of muscular, bare-chested Aryans pummeling hawk-nosed Hassidim, Bolan read:

> Warriors! The great day we have long awaited is
> upon us! We shall soon close ranks with allies
> to reclaim the Holy Land for Yahweh and destroy
> the usurpers of pseudo-Israel! With a mighty bolt
> from Heaven we shall slay them in the thousands
> and ten thousands, until none stand in our way!
> Be ready for the call to battle when it comes!
> Watch for the signs of Armageddon as the day
> draws near! The blazing lance of Faith leads
> us to victory! A world of racial purity at last!
> If you have not already pledged yourself to
> aid the cause, now is the time! History waits
> for no man! VICTORY OR DEATH!

An Arkansas post office box was listed at the bottom of the proclamation, just in case readers were inspired to send donations for the cause. Bolan shook his head. It was the standard piece of Nazi nonsense, melodrama to the max, but parts of it caught his eye. Specifically, he focused on the mention of *a mighty bolt from Heaven* and *a blazing lance*.

Those might be flights of fancy—Upshaw's takeoff on the legend that the Third Reich's leaders had possessed a magic spear of destiny that dated from the Crucifixion—or, they might refer to something else.

A supergun, for instance, out of Baghdad via Ciudad Juarez?

Bolan pocketed the flier, left the house and jogged back to his car. Five minutes later, he was on the open highway, eastbound toward St. Louis.

Bolan had no means of tracing Vernon Upshaw at the moment, but he wasn't giving up. Someone inside the ARM had answers, and they couldn't all have disappeared.

He hoped not, anyway.

For if they had, there could be hell to pay.

BROGNOLA TOOK THE CALL at home, as he was brewing coffee for his first cup of the day. He picked up automatically, not waiting for the answering machine to screen the call, and recognized the caller's voice at once.

"It's me," Bolan said. "Sorry, but it couldn't wait for office hours."

"No sweat. What's up?"

"Are we secure?"

"As modern high-tech crap can make us," Brognola said. His home and office lines were swept for taps three times a day, and built-in scramblers were installed to make sure any eavesdroppers the sweepers missed were treated to a stream of gibberish and static.

"Okay," Bolan replied. "I'm striking out here, in Ozark country. If I don't hook up with someone who can manage conversation pretty soon, we won't have anything."

"I see. What's next?"

"I'm heading west. The ARM has people in New Mexico. They may feel safe enough out there to stay at home and wait for orders. Anyway, it's worth a look."

"You need a lift?"

"If possible. Saves time spent shopping for new hardware on the other end."

"It shouldn't be a problem," Brognola said.

The 9/11 attacks had not only made things more difficult for terrorists in the United States. Airport security was still erratic, prone to errors that made headlines, but in terms of baggage screening it was almost impossible to move firearms on a commercial carrier in check-through luggage without filling out a ream of paperwork for every gun and round of ammunition registered. Brognola might've pulled some strings from Washington, but that would only turn the spotlight on clandestine ops and lead to further problems in a time when even famous senators were hassled with their names on airline "no-fly" lists.

It saved time all around to book a private charter flight or schedule Bolan for a military ride across country. There would be paperwork involved in that scenario, as well, but it was classified and might even be "lost" with help from Aaron Kurtzman's team at Stony Man Farm.

"Where are you going, in New Mexico?" Brognola asked.

"The place outside of Taos, where they want to start the Great White Nation."

"Jesus, right." It still amazed Brognola, sometimes, all the crap people believed. The fantasies they used to guide their destiny. "Okay. I'll clear you out of Fort Zumwalt, west of St. Louis, landing at Fort Bliss. That's at the wrong end of the state, I realize, but—"

"Closer than I am right now," Bolan said. "Thanks. It's fine."

"Let's use the Colonel Brandon Stone ID, since it's on file," Brognola said. "Switch back to Cooper or whatever when you're on the civvy side."

"Sounds good. I found a flier at the last place, printed for the ARM. It rambles on about a Day of Judgment coming. Pretty standard for the Nazi fringe, except it mentions bolts from Heaven and a blazing lance."

"Could be our toy," Brognola granted.

"Or, it could be crap."

"That too. Let's hope the author knew what he was writing, for a change."

"Still doesn't help us track it down," Bolan reminded him, "but if I find someone to squeeze, we may still have a shot."

"I'll keep my fingers crossed."

"It couldn't hurt," the Executioner replied. "All right, I've got a plane to catch."

"It'll be waiting for you," Brognola assured him.

There was red tape to be severed and finessed, but the big Fed's assignment to the Stony Man project included top-level clearance and a short list of phone numbers virtually guaranteed to get results. He used them sparingly, but without hesitation when a pressing need arose.

When he was finished making calls, Brognola sipped his coffee and considered what might happen if his judgment on the mission had been wrong from the beginning. What if Bolan could find nothing linking members of the ARM to the elusive supergun because there *were* no links? What if some other group of psychopathic misfits had the weapon and were plotting where to use it next, while Bolan chased the wrong suspects across the countryside?

In that case, Brognola thought, he was up one very stinky creek without a paddle to his name. It might not cost his job, but he would find it awkward to continue, in good conscience, if his judgment was that flawed. If it had led to killing and the risk of Bolan's life without due cause.

He wouldn't give up yet, of course. Bolan still had a few tricks up his sleeve, some sources to interrogate—if he could find them. Failing that, however, Brognola might need to think about another line of work.

Or maybe he should just retire. Look for a beach somewhere, where he and Helen could relax and take things easy for a change. It would be nice. No crisis calls before sunrise, scrambling young men to kill or be killed at the farthest corners of the Earth.

An end to secrets, as it were.

Someday, Brognola thought. But not yet.

5

Taos, New Mexico

As such things go, the flight was uneventful. No one poked through Bolan's bags when he arrived at Fort Zumwalt, nor did they question the U.S. Army ID he carried, naming him as Colonel Brandon Stone. The fact that he was out of uniform raised no eyebrows—or none that Bolan was allowed to glimpse, at any rate. The transport plane took off on time and landed at Fort Bliss, west of Carlsbad, on the outskirts of the White Sands Missile Range, four minutes early.

A rental car was waiting for him in the tiny town of Sunspot, and he traveled east from there on Highway 62 until he reached Artesia, then turned north and followed Highway 285 through Roswell, across the sunbaked desert to Vaughn and another junction. From there, the scorching flats turned into wooded mountain slopes, where bold Apache warriors had resisted all invaders for the best part of four hundred years. That struggle had been fierce, conducted without mercy shown by either side.

The kind of war that Bolan understood.

These days, there was a different breed of rebel in those mountains. Tax protesters and would-be secessionists, the throwbacks to a time before law reached the West, when range wars settled arguments and lynch mobs meted out revenge disguised as justice. The new breed went beyond protest to insurrection, waging ceaseless war against environmental laws, zoning, even refusing to apply for driver's licenses on the peculiar theory that their government had no authority to rule. In such an atmosphere, groups like the Aryan Resistance Movement found prime soil in which to plant their deadly seeds.

Bolan rolled into Taos at 1:30 p.m. and stopped to fill the rental's tank before proceeding to a diner on the town's main street, where he consumed a mediocre hamburger and French fries cooked to a tooth-grating crisp. Strong coffee and a slice of startling key lime pie redeemed the disappointing meal, and Bolan's tip secured directions from his waitress to the rustic suburb he was seeking.

Rebels often claimed they're "going back to nature," but the effort frequently included computer access, satellite TV and other modern frills undreamed of by pioneers who carved their homes from real-life wilderness. The place he sought, likewise, was a "survival" compound in name only. Deprivation wasn't something that its tenants wished to sample in the long run. They played war games in the woods, then trundled back to fireside couches, boozing while they argued over hidden meanings in *Mein Kampf*.

Bolan had no good reason to suppose the supergun was in Taos, but Camp Nordland was the last address he had for anything resembling an official ARM facility. Assuming that the weapon *wasn't* there, at least he had a shot at bagging someone who had heard of it and might know where to find it.

One last shot.

He made a drive-by of the rural property, saw next to nothing of the camp beyond a screen of trees, and so decided to return at nightfall for a closer look. He paid too much for a motel room, slept until a half hour before sundown, then suited up and drove back to the target site.

Bolan expected tight security after his raid in Arkansas, but he met no significant obstructions as he hiked in from an unpaved access road that marked the southern boundary of the property. He took his time, watching for guards and traps along the way, but finding neither. Only when he neared the big house, a converted hunting lodge, did men with weapons suddenly appear.

They weren't patrolling, in the standard sense. Two of them stood smoking on the front porch, rifles slung, enjoying conversation while they scanned the night from time to time. Circling around behind the house, Bolan found one more sentry there, another smoker, looking lonely as he stood beneath a light that ruined any chance of his detecting prowlers in the shadows.

Only three outside, but undoubtedly more within. And the three he could see were blocking Bolan's only means of access to the house. He hadn't planned a blitz this time, but it might be the only way to go.

In which case, he would want to kill all power to the house.

Bolan finished his circuit of the former lodge and found no evidence of any supplemental generator. If he cut the power lines outside, the house and grounds should plunge immediately into darkness. He could move then, striking while the guards were still off balance, slipping in to wreak havoc among the other lunatics in residence.

But sparing one of them, at least.

Camp Nordland's commandant was named in federal dossiers as Richard Joseph Hall, a twenty-nine-year-old with prior convictions for domestic violence and drug abuse who'd "gone straight" as a neo-Nazi following his last release from jail. His record, doubtless altered in the telling to incorporate a private struggle against ZOG, was something like a merit badge within the ARM.

He'd be the man to ask about a supergun.

Bolan retraced his steps around the house, meaning to drop the power lines some distance back into the woods. A silent burst or two from the Beretta 93-R ought to do the trick, and he could jog back to the house before his enemies recovered from the shock of sudden darkness. Time enough to drop the two guards on the porch before the folks inside could grope their way to flashlights or candles. Once he was inside—

His train of thought was interrupted when the back door opened, fifty feet in front of him, and three men left the house. A glance told Bolan one of them was under escort by the other two. They walked on either side of him and clutched his arms, which seemed to be secured behind his back. The middle man was arguing, dragging his feet, but the resistance only earned him rabbit punches to the gut and kidneys. Grunting in pain, he slumped between his escorts, leaving them to drag him toward the nearby woods.

The back door guard appeared to have no interest in the incident. He stayed put, barely noticing as two of his comrades carried a third into the trees. Bolan, meanwhile, was curious enough to veer off course and follow them.

"I NEVER SEEN A RAT this big, before," Jimmy McCarthy said.

"You never know what to expect, here in the woods," Gary Krakower replied.

Through pain and fear, it came to Randy Coyle that he had one last chance to save himself. "I'm *not* a rat," he challenged. "Yahweh knows it."

"It's a bad idea to take His name in vain," Krakower said. The punch that followed drove a spike of agony between Coyle's ribs.

"This is a huge mistake," Coyle gasped.

McCarthy sneered. "You made it, traitor."

Coyle supposed that there was nothing he could say to countermand their orders. Someone had reported him for heresy and worse, snooping around the lodge. When he was questioned, Coyle had tried to bluff it out—lie and deny—but a search of his room had turned up the digital camera with snapshots of the house and grounds, strictly forbidden by Commandant Hall. At that point, someone started calling him a Red Jew bastard, and Coyle knew that he'd been lucky to escape the room alive.

Lucky, that was, until they voted to dispose of him.

A dozen skinheads volunteered to pull the trigger, but Hall

had picked McCarthy and Krakower on the basis of experience. Both were ex-convicts, with time in maximum security, and they had spilled blood long before they found the cause. Now that their violent acts were sanctified, they had an extra zeal for mayhem, all in Yahweh's name.

"Stay sharp, traitor," McCarthy goaded him. "We're almost there."

"Came out this afternoon and got the spot all ready for you," Krakower informed him.

"I'm telling you, there's been a terrible mistake. When Hall finds out—"

"Mistake my ass," McCarthy said.

"And if it was," Krakower added, "what the hell? I figure, better safe than sorry."

"Better safe than sorry," his companion echoed.

"And then, who's next?" Coyle asked, dragging his feet to slow them in the woods. "You piss somebody off, they finger you, and then you're gone. Remember this, when you're the one on the receiving end."

"It's never gonna happen, rat," McCarthy said. "They wouldn't find a fucking camera in my room."

"It isn't *mine*," Coyle lied. The best that he could do, under the circumstances.

"Tell it to your maker, Jew Boy," Krakower suggested. "On your way to hell."

They reached a clearing in the woods, a shovel standing upright in the middle of it, as if planted in the soil. McCarthy shoved Coyle from behind, driving the captive to his knees, then placed a foot between his shoulder blades and pinned him facedown on the ground. A cold blade passed between Coyle's wrists, parting the heavy tape that held them tight together.

"You know the Auschwitz motto, don't you, rat?" McCarthy asked. "*Arbeit macht frei.*"

"That's 'work makes one free,'" Krakower reminded him. "And here's your chance to work."

"Start digging, rat," McCarthy ordered.

Coyle rose to all fours, then lurched erect. He flexed his fingers, feeling the return of circulation to his hands. He staggered toward the shovel, thinking he could use it as a weapon, but McCarthy and Krakower had stepped back out of swinging range, both watching him with pistols in their hands.

"No funny business, rat," Krakower said. "Just dig."

"My own grave, right?"

"You're catching on," McCarthy said, beaming.

Coyle straightened, squared his shoulders, let the shovel drop. "Dig it yourselves, assholes."

The skinheads blinked at each other, taken by surprise. "What did you say?" Krakower asked.

"You heard me, shithead. If you want the job done, do it yourselves."

McCarthy cocked his pistol. "If I have to dig that hole," he said, "you'll go to hell without your kneecaps. Understand?"

Coyle was surprised by his own sudden, stubborn courage. "Dead's dead," he replied. "No way I'm helping you."

"We're wasting time," Krakower growled. He raised his pistol, sighting down the barrel. "Say goodbye, rat."

Coyle stood waiting for the shot, afraid to close his eyes, and so he witnessed an extraordinary thing. Krakower's head seemed to explode, a crimson halo bursting from his skull as he pitched forward. Falling, he squeezed off a shot that whined past Coyle with room to spare and vanished whispering among the trees.

McCarthy gaped at his companion, raised his eyes toward Coyle, then recognized the truth in time to pivot on his heels, turning back toward the house. This time, Coyle heard a muffled coughing sound, before McCarthy stumbled backward and collapsed.

A part of Coyle's mind grasped what he was seeing, though he couldn't understand who was responsible for his salvation. Who in Camp Nordland would've dared—or even cared—to interrupt an execution in progress?

The man who suddenly appeared in front of Coyle was no one he had ever seen. Tall, dressed in black, with face and hands darkened, he held a pistol in his right fist, while his left clutched an assault rifle.

"Who the hell are you?" Coyle asked.

"The only friend you have right now," the stranger said.

"I see you're busy," Coyle replied, "so I'll just get out of your way and—"

"Not so fast." The pistol rose to find a level with his chest. "Before the rest of them show up, why did they want you dead?"

"A small misunderstanding. Nothing, really."

"So, you'd be no use to me."

The implication struck Coyle like a slap across the face. "I didn't say that, did I? Hey, what do you want to know?"

"Answer my question, and we'll go from there."

"They thought I was a spy," Coyle said.

"Are you?"

"I don't see what—"

"Answer."

Coyle couldn't see the trick to it. Hall wouldn't order two of his top goons eliminated for the sake of a confession, when the death sentence had already been passed. Still, if it *was* a trick—

"They're coming," the stranger said.

"Not a spy," Coyle said. "A journalist."

"Inside the ARM?"

Coyle heard the voices. "That's right. Can we get out of here? Talk somewhere else?"

"Have you learned anything worth trading?" the stranger asked.

"Plenty! I can tell you all about it when we're—"

"Over this way!" someone shouted, through the trees. Coyle saw the dancing flashlight beams.

Too late.

The stranger stowed his pistol in a shoulder holster, gripped the military rifle in both hands and turned to face the sound of the advancing hunters. Coyle saw his last chance and took it, turning in a flash and sprinting headlong through the forest.

BOLAN HAD A CHOICE to make and no more time to waste. Turning to face the hunters, he was instantly aware of his companion in the clearing running in the opposite direction, crashing through the forest with sufficient noise to let a blind man follow him. It was an irritant, but in the present circumstances Bolan couldn't blame him.

What to do?

He had three choices: stand and face the enemy, follow the fleeing prisoner, or dodge the hunters in the dark and make his own way to the house, as he had planned in the beginning.

Running was a fool's game. He would make less noise than the intended execution victim blundering ahead of him, but still enough for any hunters with a modicum of skill to follow him. It would eventually come down to a fight, and Bolan might not have a chance to pick his battleground if he was on the run. The better option, in that case, was to stand and fight, seize the advantage of surprise while the advancing gunmen reckoned they were dealing only with an unarmed man.

Evasion still remained a possibility, of course. He could sidestep the trackers, let them chase the prisoner until they either caught him or gave up the hunt, while Bolan moved on to the house. Unfortunately, since the gunshot had already roused a pack of sentries to pursuit, he knew that anyone left in the house would be on full alert, manning the doors and windows with whatever weapons were available. There was a decent chance that he could penetrate the house, but the resultant fight would nix whatever plans he had of grabbing an informant for the road.

The runner was his best hope yet for inside information, slim as that might be. But to make use of him, Bolan first had to stop the trackers, then reclaim his prisoner.

He stood and listened, marked the gunmen by their noises,

surprise and excitement mixed up with the thrill of the hunt. Their response to a single gunshot told Bolan that the execution was supposed to be silent, perhaps a knifing or garroting that wouldn't disturb any neighbors. The shot had alarmed them, and now they were coming to see what was wrong.

Bolan waited, thumbing off the Colt Commando's safety, setting the selector switch for 3-round bursts as he picked out a tree for cover, charting fields of fire. He wasn't sure yet, how many opponents he would face, but from their voices Bolan guessed there had to be four or five.

The first two blundered into view seconds later. Bolan tracked them, waiting, until three more came into his field of vision, through the trees. Three of the five were holding flashlights, pale beams sweeping back and forth, remaining nowhere long enough to truly light their way.

"Jimmy?" one of them called. "Gary?"

Bolan assumed those were the recent dead and put them just as swiftly out of mind. He framed the nearest runner in his rifle sights, noting the AR-15 carried in his one free hand, and stroked the Colt Commando's trigger.

Three 5.56 mm tumbling projectiles ripped into the skin-head's chest and dropped him thrashing in his tracks, but Bolan didn't wait to verify the kill. He was already moving on toward acquisition of his second target, squeezing off another burst when number two stopped short, gaping at his companion on the ground.

Three rounds at twenty yards had an identical effect on Bolan's second target, spinning him, his rifle flying high and wide from lifeless fingers. That one fell facedown, ignored by Bolan as he pivoted toward target number three.

Those still alive and on their feet were firing, their semiauto weapons popping in the forest, muzzle-flashes adding a strobe light effect to the remaining flashlight beams. They hadn't found a target yet, but Bolan had, nailing the third as he searched desperately for cover he would never find.

Two left, and both of them had dropped their flashlights, freeing both hands for self-defense. They had seen Bolan's muzzle-flashes, too, and so directed their defensive fire toward his position—only to discover that their mark had moved.

When Bolan fired again, it was from ten yards farther west, his bullets knocking number four into a boneless sprawl. That panicked the surviving shooter, sent him racing headlong toward the lodge, but Bolan stopped him with a rising burst that stitched three tidy holes along his spine.

More shooters would be coming, but he didn't plan to wait for them. Instead, he turned away and followed the escaping prisoner, whose distant thrashing in the woods was audible despite the combat echoes lingering in Bolan's ears.

The Executioner had no time left for subtlety or stealth. He ran all-out, closing the gap between himself and the supposed journalist, who obviously found it heavy going in the darkness, with the injuries he'd suffered from his recent beating. Dumb luck or hasty planning had him running in the general direction of the nearby access road and Bolan's rental car. It was a simple matter, then, of putting on more speed and making sure the rabbit didn't lay a hasty ambush for the hound.

Behind him, Bolan knew that anyone remaining in the ARM command post would either be scrambling to investigate the gunshots or preparing to evacuate before police arrived. In either case, his lead was adequate, if he could overtake the fugitive and—

There he was!

Instead of warning shouts or a dramatic gridiron tackle that might leave him with a fractured scapula, Bolan stopped short, raised the Commando to his shoulder and triggered a 3-round burst that rattled past the runner, gouging divots in the bark of large tree that stood slightly off center from his path.

The fleeing captive stopped short, skidding on a slick carpet of moss and leaves, collapsing backward on his outstretched hands. He glanced around, wide-eyed, in time to hear Bolan announce, "That's far enough."

"Okay, man! You're the boss!"

"Remember that," Bolan advised him, "and you just might see the sun come up tomorrow."

THEY PUT OFF ANY FURTHER conversation until they were seated in Bolan's car, rolling south out of Taos on Highway 68, toward Santa Fe.

"All right," Bolan said, when they'd covered two miles without spotting a tail, "let's start with your name."

"Randy Coyle."

"And what's your media affiliation?"

"Strictly freelance."

"Ah."

"Hey," Coyle protested, "freelancers and stringers do the bulk of all investigative journalism in America today, in case you didn't know."

"I'm glad to hear it," Bolan said. "But in the meantime, you have no credentials I can verify, and there's no reason I should swallow anything you tell me off the cuff."

"You must've grabbed me for a reason," Coyle replied.

Bolan played out the line. "I need some inside information on the ARM. You've been there, even if they stripped the shoulder patches."

Coyle reached up to touch the bare spot on his khaki sleeve. "Weird, huh?" he asked. "They've got this funky ritual and everything. Reminded me of that show *Branded*, on the Oldies Network. Ever see it?"

Bolan nodded. "*Branded* was about a man falsely accused. From what you told me earlier, they caught you red-handed."

"Yeah, well, I admit I could've done a better job hiding the camera."

"But no one sent you in to do a job for any recognized network or newspaper?"

"I *told* you, strictly freelance. When I'm finished with the story, I expect a bidding war."

"It's hard to write a story from a shallow grave."

"Yeah, that's a catch I hadn't figured on. I owe you one, Mr. ...?"

"Cooper," Bolan replied. "Matt Cooper."

"Not *Detective* Cooper? Maybe *Agent* Cooper?"

"Nope. I'm freelance, just like you."

"Except I don't kill people."

"You're complaining, now?"

"Far from it, friend," Coyle said. "As far as I'm concerned, it's *never* a good day to die."

"Hold that thought," Bolan suggested, "while you tell me why you chose to infiltrate the ARM."

"I've always been intrigued by right-wing lunatics," Coyle said. "The Aryan Resistance Movement is the biggest, baddest Nazi clique in the U.S. They make the Klan and Posse Comitatus look like poseurs. Plus, I have score to settle."

"Meaning?"

"Bernie Levinson, my best friend at Columbia back in the day, was working on a piece about the ARM last year, on staff with the St. Louis *Post-Dispatch*. Before the first installment of his series ran, somebody broke into his place and cut his throat, trashed his computer, made off with his paper files."

"You think it was the ARM?"

"It wasn't the Salvation Army, pal. Of course, St. Louie's finest found an ounce of weed in Bernie's flat and wrote it off as 'drug-related.' I'll be working on them next, believe me."

"If you live that long," Bolan replied.

"Why shouldn't I?"

"How quickly you forget that shallow grave."

"Come on! I don't know who the hell you are or what you're up to, but I don't believe you saved me from the Junior League Gestapo just to take me out yourself."

"You're right. It was the ARM I had in mind."

Coyle smirked. "How would they find me?"

"How'd they find your friend?"

"Bernie got careless."

"So did you."

"Touché. So, what do you suggest?"

"School me on what you've learned about the inner workings of the ARM, answer some questions, and I'll see that you're protected while you write your story."

"Just like that?" Coyle asked, suspicion heavy in his tone. "Give up my info on a handshake?"

"The risk is mine," Bolan said. "If I act on information you provide and it's a scam, someone could suffer for it."

"Meaning me?"

"You wouldn't be the first. Maybe the last."

"So, I'm a *prisoner*?"

"You were a prisoner condemned when I first saw you. Think of this as trading up."

"And if I don't play?"

Bolan shrugged. "I turn around and drop you with your friends. They seemed upset to see you leave."

"This is extortion! Blackmail!"

"I prefer to call it symbiosis," Bolan said. "The choice is yours."

"Some choice."

"The last one you were offered came to dying with your kneecaps, or without."

"You've got a point."

"So, what's your answer?"

"It's a go, on one condition."

"Which would be?"

"I get to ask some questions, too. Starting with who you are and why you're shooting Nazis in New Mexico."

"No trade," Bolan said. "You're concerned about a byline. I'm concerned with life and death."

"I figured that out when you shot the Hitler Youth, back there."

"No trade," Bolan repeated.

"Fine. No trade, no deal."

Bolan stood on the brake, swerving his car to the highway's shoulder. "Right," he said. "You're on your own."

Coyle blanched by dashboard light. "Hey, what the hell? We're in the middle of nowhere!"

The night pressed close around them. Bolan killed his headlights to accentuate the darkness. "I don't see any Nazis," he told Coyle. "You've got a fair head start. They probably won't find you for a few days, anyway. Unless you left something behind that puts them on your trail."

"This sucks!"

"That's life."

"All right, then, dammit! Ask your questions."

"You can fill me in about your tenure as a pseudo-Nazi while we drive," Bolan said. "Anything that comes to mind along the way, I'll interrupt."

"Terrific. Where should I begin?"

"Where every story starts," the Executioner replied. "At the beginning."

6

"If you want to start at the beginning," Coyle stated, "we have to go back to my folks. They're sixties people, dig it? Pop went down from Berkeley to the Freedom Summer project, back in '64. He knew those guys the Klan killed. You remember *Mississippi Burning?*"

Bolan said, "It rings a bell."

"Okay. Mom was a hippie chick, I guess you'd say, although she came from money in New York. They hooked up in Chicago, at the '68 convention riots. That was huge, I guess, back in the day."

Bolan was silent at the wheel, waiting.

"Between them," Coyle went on, "they taught me not to sit around and watch while things go wrong. It's better to pitch in and fix them."

"Or at least report the problem," Bolan said.

"Exactly! How can people mobilize in ignorance? How can they help themselves, if they don't know a threat exists?"

"You understand," the warrior said, "that when I say 'the beginning,' I don't mean the Book of Genesis?"

"Okay. I told you about Bernie, how the cops blew off his murder, right? So, it occurred to me that if the boys in blue were doing *nada,* maybe I should take a shot and see what I come up with."

"Crack the case and grab a byline in the process."

"Why not? Woodward and Bernstein brought down Tricky

Dick. John Hersey blew the whistle on My Lai. Mike Wallace had the smoking thing, until his boss spiked the story, then he—"

"Focus," Bolan ordered.

"Right. My point is, there's nothing wrong with what I do."

"You haven't told me what that is, yet."

"Simple—I investigate and I report. Bernie had shown me bits and pieces of his story on the ARM, knowing my academic interest in the brown-shirt boys, so I already had a leg up on the story when he died. His files were lost, but I retraced some of his legwork and developed sources of my own. The more I learned about the ARM, the more I've come to see it as a threat, the kind of thing courts call a 'clear and present danger.'"

"But you didn't have enough to write the story from outside?" Bolan asked.

"Sure, I could have," Coyle replied, watching the rearview mirror apprehensively for headlights, "but it wouldn't be the best work I can do. Go for the inside view whenever possible. That's where you find the dirt—and gold."

"Was that the way your friend worked?"

"Bernie?" Coyle shook his head. "No, he was pretty much straight-arrow. Oh, he'd pay informants now and then, use documents of questionable provenance, but going under cover from the *Post-Dispatch* was out of bounds. Besides, the ARM wouldn't have let him in. He looked too Jewish."

Bolan pinned Coyle with a sidelong glance that made him wince. "Hey, it's a fact of life, okay? I'm being honest, here. You wouldn't sent a black guy to infiltrate the KKK, would you?"

"I doubt it," Bolan said.

"All right, then. Where was I?"

"Finding the dirt and gold inside the ARM."

"Not quite. I did my research first, went to some rallies, read the literature, if you can call it that. I waited eight months after Bernie's funeral before I filed my application to become a junior jackboot warrior."

"If you went in with that kind of flippant attitude," Bolan said, "I'm surprised they didn't try to kill you earlier."

"Give me some credit, will you? Any good investigative journalist is also an accomplished actor. Anyway, your basic Nazi is a simpleminded goon. Buy him a beer, repeat the 'Red-kike-nigger' mantra, and he'll be your friend for life."

"They saw through you, back there," Bolan reminded him.

"I had a momentary lapse, okay? It happens."

"And you've had your second chance. Go on."

"I'm going. Jeez! My point is that I did my homework first, before I signed on with the ARM to get the inside look. I learned their history, built dossiers on leaders past and present, researched court cases, reviewed the group's mythology—"

"How's that?" Bolan interrupted.

"What?"

"You said, 'the group's mythology.' What do you mean by that?"

"Extremist groups often surround themselves with bullshit stories that assume a kind of urban-legend status. Nazis are the worst, for that. You may not know it, but the Hitler gang in Germany grew from a cult that called itself the Thule Society. They studied Nordic mumbo-jumbo, runes and whatnot, mixed it up with Satanism and some crap about a hollow Earth—and, presto! They're the Master Race. I'm telling you, Nazis are lunatics."

"What relevance does that have to the ARM?" Bolan asked.

"*Nazis,* man! They're all the same. The stories change, but they're a superstitious bunch of idiots. Remember George Lincoln Rockwell?"

"Founder of the American Nazi Party," Bolan said.

"Bingo! Before a sidekick snuffed him, back in '67, Rockwell proposed a merger of his group with the Church of Satan. And get this, the devil-worship crowd blew him off. Even *they* know Nazis are nuts. Same thing with the ARM."

"Give me an example."

"Well...you know Curt Walgren, right?"

Bolan nodded. "Reigning honcho of the ARM."

"The very same. They figure he's some kind of Superman."

"You're talking Nietzsche, right?"

Coyle shook his head emphatically. "I'm talking Man of Steel, as in the comics—or, should that be graphic novels."

"I don't follow you," Bolan said.

"Four years back, he almost went the way of Rockwell. Had a beef with one of his subordinates who couldn't let it go. The guy pulled a gun on him, plugged Curt twice at point-blank range before the bodyguards can take him down."

"I take it he survived."

"Survived? I'd say so, yeah. They rushed him to the hospital, death's door, the whole nine yards. That night, he vanished from Intensive Care without a trace. Next morning, bright and early, Walgren grants an interview to some hick public-access TV channel in Missouri. Takes his shirt off for the cameras. *Voilà!* No wounds."

"So, he wore Kevlar," Bolan said.

"I think the surgeons would've noticed. Anyway, I bought a copy of his file, complete with X-rays. He was hit, all right."

Bolan frowned. "He's not bulletproof."

"Guess not. Maybe he just heals overnight?"

"Impossible."

"You'd think so, right? But, then again, most people can't bilocate, either."

"Say again?"

"You heard me, man. According to the ARM's mythology, Walgren has power to appear in two different places at the same time."

"You buy this nonsense?" Bolan asked his passenger. Another glance at Coyle by dashboard light revealed a solemn face, no smirking.

"Hey," the reporter said, "I'd be tickled pink to puncture that particular balloon. It would be better than exposing criminal activity."

"How's that?" Bolan asked.

"Think about it. Movements like the ARM and KKK draw their recruits from a subculture where extremism and paranoia are the norm. They want street fighters, night-riders, bomb-throwers. It's a crazy fact of life that if I prove the ARM killed Bernie Levinson, if some of them do time or get the chair for it, that news would *help* them find the sort of maniacs they're looking for. The scum they thrive on."

"But a simple scam would throw them off?" Bolan inquired.

Coyle nodded. "Sure it would. Your basic Nazi thinks he holds the secrets of the universe, from Adam and creation to the final race war for control of Planet Earth. Show him that the very leaders he respects have played him for a sucker, and you wound the moron's pride. His rage is redirected from minorities to those who've tricked him. At the very least, some of the goons would quit and find another litter box to play in."

"So, let me get this straight," Bolan said. "You went after Walgren and the ARM for murdering your friend, but you're content to write an exposé about some dime store sleight of hand routine?"

"Content?" Coyle sneered. "I'll be *content* when every one of them is rotting in a prison cell. But in the meantime, I'll do what I can with what I've got, okay?"

"And what is that, exactly?" Bolan prodded him.

"Not much."

"Explain."

"All right, the bilocating thing," Coyle said. "I figured it should be an easy thing to figure out, you know? Somebody lies about it, maybe Walgren spreads the word himself, through underlings. The photos scuttled that idea."

"Photos?"

"Uh-huh. The fact is that on two occasions in the past twelve months, Walgren's been photographed in circumstances that are strange, to say the least."

"I'm listening."

"Okay. June third, last year, he gave the basic Nazis-hate-the government address to ten or twelve supporters and about four hundred hecklers in Des Moines. Plenty of photos published, and it made TV that night, because a pair of skinheads jumped a rabbi in the crowd. Film at eleven, as they say."

"It sounds routine," Bolan replied.

"It was, until the *Arm of Yahweh* ran an article in its July issue, with photos of Walgren at some booze fest in Miami, taken on June third."

"What time of day?" Bolan asked.

"See, that was my question, too. Hop on a plane from Iowa to sunny Florida, what would it be? Four hours? Maybe six, at the outside?"

"Sounds right," Bolan agreed.

"Except, the witnesses I interviewed and the internal evidence from half a dozen photos indicates that the Miami snaps were taken within *thirty minutes* of the rant in Iowa."

"Internal evidence?"

"I had the pics enhanced and analyzed, okay? Walgren was in a bar. One of the patrons in the background had a newspaper, which showed the date. A wall clock nailed the time. My interviews and common sense confirmed the photos had been taken in the afternoon, and not twelve hours later, when the place was closed."

"All right," Bolan said, thinking rapidly. "So, Walgren's even more like Hitler than you thought. He has a double."

"Way ahead of you," Coyle said. "While I was shelling out my hard-earned money to the photo lab, I had them do comparisons of both the rally photos and the beer snaps with other photographs of Walgren, taken since he surfaced as the ARM's white knight. I won't pretend to understand the process, but the experts say there's not a silly millimeter's difference between the faces in those photographs."

"A double, like I said," Bolan repeated.

"An *exact* double, the same in every microscopic detail?"

"You can't say that, from the face alone."

"It's close enough, believe me. I've got documents from analysts that would stand up in court, if we were trying to identify a corpse or fugitive."

"What are you saying, then?"

"I told you there were *two* occasions in the past year, where photographers caught Walgren in two places at once."

"*Apparently*," Bolan corrected him.

"Uh-huh. Just listen, will you? April ninth of this year, Walgren took a trip to Mexico, crossing the border at El Paso."

"Oh?" Bolan relaxed his grip on the car's steering wheel with an effort.

"Vacation, whatever," Coyle said. "Anyway, they've got cameras all over the main border crossing. Immigration, DEA, the war on terror, yada-yada. Damn near everyone is photographed, coming and going."

"So?"

"So, Walgren got his picture taken at 10:43 a.m., crossing the border in a Ford Cortina. Ninety minutes later, they snapped him again, going across in a red Toyota."

"What's the mystery?" Bolan asked. "He changed cars before he came back to the States."

"He wasn't *coming back*, okay? Both photos caught him heading south. He didn't cross back into the U.S. between the times when they were taken. I've reviewed the film, believe me, and there's nothing."

"Are you claiming he never came back?" Bolan asked.

"Not *that* day, at *that* crossing. Cameras picked him up again next morning, reentering the States at Port Hancock. That's thirty-odd miles—"

Bolan stopped him. "I know where it is."

"So, you see what I mean?"

Bolan decided it was time to take a chance. "Let's leave the voodoo for a minute," he replied, "and look at something else."

"Such as?"

"What can you tell me about secret weapons?"

7

"The secret weapon," Coyle said, smiling. "It's part of standard Nazi myth and bullshit, predating the Third Reich. Heinrich Himmler spent millions and killed hundreds, maybe thousands, trying to find the original Ark of the Covenant, you know."

He saw the look on Bolan's face and smiled. "You thought all that was just a movie, right? Of course, they never *found* it in real life, assuming it ever existed, but the SS never gave up. Himmler used slave labor to build himself a black-magic ritual chamber at Wewelsburg, in an old castle dungeon, hoping demons would help the Fatherland conquer the world."

"It didn't work," Bolan said.

"There's a shocker. Nazi secret weapons never work. Hitler was close to finishing an atom bomb, before he called it off. Same thing with jet airplanes, assault rifles, robotic tanks. He had some great ideas but scrapped them all, because he was a nut."

"I'm talking about Walgren and the ARM right now," Bolan reminded him, "not Germany in 1945."

"I hear you, but it's all the same. Nazis daydream. They fantasize. Jesus, they're so hooked on the Master Race nonsense that they convince themselves they're geniuses. Whip out one harebrained scheme after another for superweapons, medical experiments to purify the race, you name it. On the rare occasions when they have a workable idea, they almost never follow through. It's one advantage that the sane folk have over the lunatics."

"I'm not suggesting they've invented anything," Bolan said,

"but if some groundbreaking weapon was provided to them, I assume they'd use it."

"Hell, yes," Coyle agreed. "They're always looking for the magic thunderbolt."

"Say what?"

The look on Bolan's face was stark, almost cadaverous by dashboard light. Coyle hesitated for a moment, then replied, "I said, they're always looking for the magic thunderbolt."

"Why do you call it that?" Bolan said.

"*I* don't," Coyle informed him. "*They* do. It's symbolic, see." Coyle brought a hand up to his shoulder and was reminded that the goons had stripped his patches from the brown shirt he still wore. "The lightning bolt was an insignia of the original SS, okay? Blitzkrieg, the wrath of Thor, whatever. Anyway, after the war, a lot of neo-Nazi factions ripped it off for flags, armbands and so forth. In the States, a bunch of southern nitwits known as the Columbians first used it, back in 1946. They called their newspaper *The Thunderbolt*. Dozens of other groups have picked it up since then, the ARM included, as a sign of solidarity with the Third Reich."

"You're talking flags and shoulder patches here, not weapons," Bolan said.

"But it's a concept, see? The thunderbolt symbolizes power, striking from above to smite the movement's enemies. If you assume that power is divine, and that it values human effort, then why shouldn't it provide a superweapon to the faithful."

"How long were you inside the ARM?"

The change-up startled Coyle, forcing him to think about his answer. "Seven months, nine days," he said at last, "from my initiation through tonight. Guess I'm retired."

"I understand that ARM initiations commonly involve some kind of criminal activity," Bolan said.

"That's a fact."

"So, what was yours."

"I got off relatively easy," Coyle replied. "One of their strike teams took me out to vandalize a synagogue. It's not important where. They trashed the place—*we* did—and then went out gay-bashing. My illustrious comrades were so strung out on hate and booze by then, they didn't notice when I hung back on the beatings. One of them was carrying a camcorder, but he stayed focused on the action, while I hopped around and did a lot of yelling for the sound track."

Coyle lapsed into silence then, clearly ashamed of his complicity but willing to defend it if attacked. Instead, Bolan switched tacks again, surprising him once more.

"So, in your seven months and nine days as a Nazi, you heard nothing to suggest the 'thunderbolt' might be some kind of real-life weapon?"

"Hey, I never said that. Nazis *talk,* okay? Most of them suffer from a kind of verbal diarrhea that's incurable. They blather day and night about drinking and screwing, fighting and killing, explosives and weapons. That includes the so-called thunderbolt."

"Do they discuss it as a real thing?" Bolan pressed him.

"More as something they anticipate, except—" Coyle hesitated, blinking. "Hey! You think the thunderbolt exists?"

Bolan ducked the question. "What I'm asking is if *you* experienced or witnessed anything during your seven months, nine days inside the ARM to make *you* think it's real."

Coyle thought about it, frowning, looking past their headlights at the dark highway. "Now that you mention it, there was more talk about it in the past few weeks. Some of the skinheads rambling on. 'The thunderbolt is coming,' or whatever. Crazy talk."

"Which skinheads?" Bolan asked.

"Mainly the two you shot tonight, or should I say the first two? Krakower and McCarthy. They were always long on mouth and short on brains."

Bolan was silent, concentrating on the road and private thoughts. Coyle thought he understood the change in mood.

"So, what? You're sorry that you killed them now?" he asked. "You're wishing that they'd wasted me, instead?"

"If they knew anything, I could've used it," Bolan said. "It's too late, anyway. Spilt milk."

"Gee, thanks. Just wipe me up and throw away the paper towel." Coyle sulked.

"Stop whining, will you?" Bolan said. "You're still alive."

Coyle's instinct for a story brought him back on track. "But I was right," he said. "You think the thunderbolt is real!"

"It may be," Bolan said. "And if it is, we're in for a world of hurt."

Bolan refused to answer any further questions as they motored through the night. Eventually, Coyle lapsed into moody silence, then dozed off and started snoring, slumped against the window on his side.

Bolan had no clear destination in mind, no further targets on his list. He needed rest, and to touch base with Hal Brognola, maybe tap resources at the Farm before he risked another major step. With that in mind, he started watching road signs, following billboard directions to a motel set back from the highway, screened by pines.

It wouldn't qualify as safe, since anyone could come along and read the sign, then swing by for a look around, but Bolan reckoned it beat sleeping in the car. Walls would provide at least some measure of security, and there'd be ways he could restrain Coyle in a motel room that kept him out of reach of Bolan's weapons, without having to hog-tie him.

Tires crunched on gravel as they left the two-lane highway for a narrow access road, then left that road in turn to navigate a stingy, unpaved driveway. Coyle woke as they neared a long, single-story structure, featuring a neon sign that read Vacancy, with the *C* burned out. "God," he muttered, "it's the Bates Motel."

"Avoid the shower," the Executioner cautioned. "You'll be fine."

Before Coyle could protest, Bolan palmed a pair of handcuffs and secured Coyle's left arm to the steering wheel, then pocketed the car keys.

"Sit tight."

"As if I've got a choice," Coyle groused.

The office door was locked but had a doorbell mounted on it, with a small hand-lettered sign inviting would-be guests to Ring any Time. Bolan did so, heard buzzing inside, and then waited a moment. His trigger finger was extended for another jab, when lights came on inside the office, and a sixty-something man with spiked hair and a faded bathrobe peered out from a door behind the check-in counter.

Bolan let the man observe him for a moment, then prepared to press the bell again. At that, the snowy-haired curmudgeon scowled and hobbled forward, moving with a gait that fell somewhere between a shuffle and a limp.

"It's late, or early," the man told Bolan after he'd unlocked the door.

"Your sign says—"

"I know what it says. I wrote it, didn't I?"

"I wouldn't know," Bolan replied, putting a touch of steel into his tone. "You have a vacant room, or not?"

"Vacant's the only kind I got, these days." The old man hobbled back around the counter and produced a registration card, together with a ballpoint pen. "How many in your party?"

"Two," Bolan said.

"Man and wife?"

"Is this a motel, or a church?" Bolan inquired.

The man considered a reply, but then apparently thought better of it. "Forty dollars for the night," he said. "That means tonight, what's left of it."

Bolan handed the man two twenties and filled out the card, using the Cooper alias, his rental's license number and a mythical address in Santa Fe.

"Phone number at the bottom."

"It's unlisted," Bolan said. "You won't be calling me."

The old man glowered, then retrieved a brass key with a plastic fob that bore the number 9. "Room's out the door and on your left. Our checkout time is ten o'clock in the a.m. Stay on past ten, you owe for another night."

Bolan simply nodded and took the key.

The old man had a clear view of the car as Bolan climbed inside and pulled down to the parking spot outside his room. He couldn't have seen Bolan unlock the handcuffs, but there was outrage on his long face when he saw two men step from the car and pass across the threshold. Bolan lingered in the doorway for a moment and saw the manager head back to bed.

"Old fart might call the cops," Coyle said, half-smiling. "Two men in a room. It's freaking scandalous."

"You've got the wrong decade," Bolan replied.

"I'll bet you spoiled his sleep, at least. He's tossing in his bed right now, imagining some kind of debauchery in progress."

Bolan placed his duffel bag of weapons on the floor beside one of the room's two beds. He chose the bed closer to door and windows, just in case trouble should find them during what remained of an exhausting night.

He checked the bathroom for escape routes, found its tiny window welded shut by rust and ancient paint. "It's all yours," Bolan said, "but make it count. I'm cuffing you tonight."

"So macho," Coyle retorted. "Listen—"

"The alternative is shooting, if you run. I'd try to hit your legs, but being sleepy, in the dark and all—"

"I'll take the cuffs," Coyle said.

A quarter-hour later, they were settled in the darkness, lying in their twin beds with a cheap nightstand and two feet of drab carpeting between them. Bolan had the Beretta under his pillow, while the Colt Commando leaned against his headboard, on the side away from Coyle. The journalist was handcuffed by his right wrist, to the bed frame, which necessitated lying on his side.

His voice came from the dark to Bolan's ears. "Hey, man. You really think the thunderbolt exists?"

Bolan considered his reply, then said, "I know it does. In fact, it's already been used."

He heard Coyle try to sit upright in bed, before the handcuffs pulled him back and down. "You don't mean—"

"We can talk about it in the morning. Sleep now, while you can."

"Sleep now? You tell me psycho-Nazis have a secret weapon and they're using it, and expect me to sleep? Jesus!"

"I can promise you," Bolan replied, "He doesn't have a thing to do with it."

"That's cute, but what about—"

"You need a gag to match the cuffs?"

Coyle muttered something unintelligible, tried to turn away from Bolan, but the cuffs restrained him. "Goddamn Bates Motel," he said.

"Shut up and go to sleep," Bolan advised.

"I'll sleep, dammit. But you'd best believe I'll want some answers in the morning."

Bolan closed his weary eyes, thinking he wasn't the only one.

8

"Again? New Mexico, this time? How is that possible?"

Embarrassed, Barry James could only shrug. "I'm not—"

"It was rhetorical, all right?" Curt Walgren snapped. "That means I don't expect an answer, get it?"

"Right. Okay."

He paced the twelve-by-ten-foot office cubicle while James stood in the corner, tracking him with nervous eyes. Walgren was near the detonation point, and James had learned to read the warning signs.

Stopping to face his second in command, Walgren demanded, "Tell me, then. How is this possible? Both of our main facilities attacked, two days and—what?—five hundred miles apart? How does that happen, Barry?"

"Strictly speaking, we can't say Camp Nordland was attacked. They were supposed to be disposing of that mole, the news guy, but he got away from them somehow. Next thing Hall knows, he's got seven dead men and the spy's in the wind."

"Which is another problem that we're stuck with, now," Walgren replied. "One simple job, and Hall can't get it right. But tell me, Barry, do you really think it's a coincidence, this shit all happening at once? I mean, what are the odds?"

"Is that rhetorical?" James asked hesitantly.

"No. Go get a fucking calculator, will you? Work it out. Jesus, of course it was rhetorical."

"Sorry."

"Two days, two states, two hits. What's the connection there? My gut tells me there has to be one."

"If I had to guess—"

"Go on."

"I'd say the damned newspaper guy, whatever he's supposed to be. He joined the Movement seven months ago, and you can bet he did his homework first. He must have contacts, maybe on the left, maybe in ZOG. We need to think of who he's really working for and what he wants."

"That's obvious," Walgren replied. "What do they all want, Barry?"

"To destroy us," James replied without a hint of hesitation.

"Right. Between the ridicule in print, harassment in the courts, and every filthy trick the Jews can think of to distract or wound us, they believe we've been emasculated. Do you know what that means, Barry?"

"Cut our balls off."

"Absolutely right. They think we're beaten, on the run. And then, just when we're ready to unleash the Thunderbolt against them, after one trial run, we've got commando raids and dead troops piling up like cord wood. Do you think that's a coincidence?

"No way."

"No way is goddamned right! The spy—what was his name, again?"

"He put 'John Akroyd' on his application, but Hall found a Missouri driver's license in his shit at Nordland, with the camera. It says he's Randall Arthur Coyle."

"Address?"

"St. Louis. We've got three men on the way to check it out, see if there's anything to tell us who he's working for."

"Okay," Walgren said. "There's a chance, however slim, that Mr. Asshole Akroyd-Coyle isn't involved with the attacks per se. I know it's stretching, but his rescue or escape could be coincidental, if the raiders hit just when he was supposed to get the chop."

"I don't know," James replied. "It's pretty—"

"Thin, I know. More likely, he's in league up to his god-damned eyes with whoever's been hitting us. But then, I have to ask myself, why would they hit Camp Yahweh first, instead of helping Coyle, in New Mexico."

"He's out," James said. "The bastard got away."

"But it was close. Unless Hall's shitting us big-time, five minutes either way, and Coyle would've been in the ground. We're sure he had no way to signal out, coordinate a rescue in the nick of time. So, take your pick—either the snatch was a coincidence, or else they hit Camp Yahweh first because they're really after something else."

"Like what?" James asked, then flushed. "Oh, shit!"

"The Thunderbolt," Walgren confirmed. "What else?"

"But if they know we have it, why'd they hit the camps?"

"Because they don't know where we have it, Barry. It's exactly as I planned, if you recall—except for the attacks, that is. I thought they'd come with warrants, asking questions. That means airtime. I was counting on it, as a springboard for the main event."

"They don't need warrants if they're not official," James reminded him.

"You still think it's Mossad or someone from the JDL?"

"Why not?"

"All right, look into it. Use any sources we have left, and let them know it's urgent. Meanwhile, we need to arrange another demonstration."

"With the Thunderbolt?"

"Our first test was successful," Walgren said, "but if we stop now, our opponents will assume we're beaten. We're on the offensive, Barry, pushing forward to confront the enemy. Setbacks can't stop us now. We persevere and we prevail."

"I'll get the team together for a briefing."

"Make it six o'clock."

"Will do."

"I'll see you then."

When James was gone, Walgren retreated to his private room and stood before his mirror image once again. "It's bad news," the reflection said.

"You heard?"

"I always hear."

"I've taken care of it."

"Have you?"

"If you heard everything—"

"It could be dangerous, another strike."

"War's always dangerous. We have the Thunderbolt."

"Against an army?"

"No, against specific targets. I don't care how many men the other side can field. Their chiefs are always vulnerable."

"So am I."

"Don't worry. I'll take care of everything."

"I'll help you."

"I expect no less."

"The day of victory, almost at hand!"

"It's close, now. I can feel it."

"When my enemies will tremble!"

"When they'll die!"

"In Yahweh's name."

Curt Walgren smiled into his own eyes and replied, "Amen."

9

Breakfast was eggs and pancakes in a roadside diner, at the crack of dawn. After a pit stop in the men's room, Cooper standing by in case he tried to run, Coyle joined his savior-captor in the car. More highway stretching out in front of them, facing the sun as they drove eastward, toward the Texas panhandle.

Coyle broke the silence after they'd been on the road for fifteen minutes. "So, is this the way you really want to play it?" he inquired. "Watching me pee and cuffing me to motel beds at night?"

"I have a call to make this morning," Bolan told him. "You'll be taken care of, soon."

"What's that supposed to mean?"

"Protective custody until I'm finished, more than likely."

"What about my story?"

The Executioner shrugged. "That's not my call."

"Damn right, it's not! The First Amendment—"

"Didn't save your butt last night."

"Is that your theory? Pull me out of one tight spot and you can censor what I write for the rest of my life?"

"Your life's not over, yet. We're taking one day at a time."

"This is illegal, man. The whole damned thing."

"You're catching on."

A sudden thought struck Coyle. "Hey, wait a minute. This protective custody, is that like jail?"

"I doubt it," Bolan said.

"But either way, I'm off the story, right? That's what you're saying."

"You were off the story when your skinhead buddies found the camera in your bag," the warrior replied. "Your inside angle's blown, in case you missed it. Welcome to reality."

"I mean part two," Coyle answered. "What about the part where Walgren and his goons get put away? You're leaving me with half a story, man. It isn't worth jack shit without an ending."

"Sorry." Bolan didn't sound it.

"Right." Coyle hit upon another angle of attack. "You know, I'm not just excess baggage, here. I could be helpful, if you let me."

"In return for some kind of exclusive, I suppose?"

"Well..."

"Not a chance."

"You want to crack the ARM, right? So do I. What's wrong with some cooperation in a common cause?"

"Nothing, if it presents some benefit and doesn't make things worse," Bolan stated.

"You don't think I can be helpful?"

Stony silence from the driver, as the road unwound behind them.

"Okay, tell me this," Coyle said. "What's your next stop?"

"Nice try."

"I mean, do you have anything on tap at all? Another target? Someone you can question, if you're looking for the so-called magic thunderbolt?"

"I guess you've got a list of options in your pocket," Bolan challenged.

"Nope." Coyle grinned and tapped his temple with an index finger. "It's right here."

"You've got an address for me, on the supergun?"

"As if. I'm not the one who thinks it's real, remember? But I know a member of the movement who could tell you if it is."

"So, give."

"It's quid pro quo, amigo. Share and share alike."

"What are you asking for a name and address?"

"What it's worth. No more, no less."

"You're leaving that to me?" Bolan asked.

Coyle thought. "Okay," he finally said. "Let's say a ride-along to see what happens when you find the man. We can negotiate whatever happens after that."

Bolan considered it, then shook his head. "No good. Even if you have valid information, you'd be in the way. I'd have to spend the whole time making sure you didn't stop a bullet."

"That's a crock. I just spent seven months inside the ARM. You think that wasn't dangerous? It damn near got me killed!"

The words had barely passed Coyle's lips when he regretted them. Bolan glanced over at him, then returned his flat gaze to the road.

"That only proves you're careless," the driver said. "And the full responsibility was yours. If you get smoked on my watch, operating on the wrong side of the law with my okay, it's an entirely different story."

"Why? You think I'll try and sue you when I'm dead?"

"You're a civilian," Bolan told him. "Irresponsible, untrained and uncontrollable outside my line of sight unless restrained. Collaboration builds on trust. Strike three."

"You want trust?" Coyle replied. "Try this for size. I'll let you have the name and address *first*. You check it out, confirm it, then decide if you can use my help. Nothing to lose, right?"

"Fair enough," Bolan said. "Give."

"All right! You want to find a superweapon, ask the movement's armorer. He's—"

"Neville Hoskins," Bolan interrupted, rattling off the low-rent address in Poplar Bluff, Missouri. "I was there two days ago. He's in the wind."

"No forwarding address?"

"It must've slipped his mind."

"Well, there you are." Coyle smiled. "Good thing for you I happened by."

"Explain."

"I've got the address for his home-away-from-home. A couple of them, actually. Turn up the heat, and Nellie does a fade. But he still keeps in touch."

"If this is crap—"

"Hey, would I lie to you?" Coyle said

"Just once."

"I hear you, man. Is it a deal?"

"I'll think about it."

"Great! Will that take long?

"As long as it takes."

"Because, I'm thinking that the natives may be restless. Looking for some payback, if you get my drift. Settle some scores, whatever."

Bolan drove in silence for another mile. "I need to make a call," he said

"IT'S ME," the voice announced.

A feeling of relief washed over Hal Brognola, tempered instantly with caution. Bolan calling, talking, meant he was alive, most likely well. The dark cloud to that silver lining was that he most likely needed help, or was about to warn Brognola of some action he had planned, a scheme that might either pay off tremendously or blow up in his face. Catastrophe or triumph were the choices commonly relayed over Brognola's private line.

"You sound good," he told Bolan. "Are you making any headway?"

"Possibly. I picked up someone at the camp last night. The skinheads had him scheduled for a dirt nap, but I talked them out of it."

So that explained it. CNN had run a short spot on its *Headline News*, reporting seven dead from gunshot wounds at "an alleged neo-Nazi encampment" near Taos. After the quick flight west, he'd known Bolan had to be involved, but there'd been no more details by the time he left for work.

And waiting was a bitch.

"You must've been persuasive," Brognola replied.

"I held my own."

And then some, right. "So, who's the foundling?" Brognola asked.

"Claims to be a freelance journalist," Bolan explained. "I need a background check to find out if he's playing straight. There should be bylines somewhere, if he's working."

"What's the name?" Brognola asked.

"He goes by Randy Coyle. The full name should be Randall Arthur Coyle."

"And if it's not?"

"We'll need to have another chat, Randy and I."

Brognola knew what that meant, and he wouldn't want to be on the receiving end of Bolan's wrath. "You think this guy can help you?" he inquired.

"It's possible. He spent some time inside the ARM before they caught him snooping and decided to get rid of him. He claims to know where Neville Hoskins hides when there's a heat wave."

"You believe him?"

Bolan hesitated for a moment, then replied, "I'm leaning that way. Even if he fudged his résumé, he obviously hates the ARM. Claims they took out a friend of his some time ago, another newsie."

"Details?"

"Coyle calls him Bernie Levinson. Staff writer for the *Post-Dispatch*, out of St. Louis. Maybe murdered by a home invader, in the middle of a series on the ARM."

"And they were friends?" Brognola asked.

"Classmates, way back," Bolan replied.

"Coyle says."

"That's right."

"If true, he could be volatile."

"I'm watching it."

"Okay. No word, I take it, on our toy?"

"Words are all I've got, so far," Bolan said. "Seems the piece plays into Aryan mythology about a superweapon from the gods, or some such thing. They talk about using a thunderbolt against their enemies, but Coyle saw nothing of it while he was inside the group."

"Could be another urban legend," the man from Justice suggested.

"Maybe. But a legend didn't blow those trucks in Utah."

"No. I'll run these names ASAP. You have a landline number where I can call back in fifteen minutes, give or take?"

Bolan read off ten numerals, while Brognola transcribed them on a notepad. "Got it," he said. "Fifteen minutes, tops."

He broke the link to Bolan, dialing through at once to Stony Man. Kurtzman entered the names and sparse details into his bank of cutting-edge computers, making small talk with his boss in Washington while computer hardware worked its magic. Eight minutes and twenty seconds later, Brognola's computer screen displayed details on Randall Arthur Coyle and Bernard Joseph Levinson that the two men themselves— if both had been alive—likely couldn't recall.

Brognola skimmed it while he dialed the Texas prefix Bolan had provided, waited through two rings before the hard voice in his ear declared, "Still here."

"You want a rundown or an e-mail?" he asked Bolan.

"Run it down."

"Okay. Your man appears to be legit, as far as we can tell. Studied his craft in New York, at Columbia, where he shared classes and a dorm with Levinson. Looks like they split up after graduation, back in 1995. Levinson worked for a couple papers, did all right, before he wound up at the *Post-Dispatch* in '99. Coyle got laid off from the San Francisco *Chronicle* his fifth week on the job—no details, there—and switched to alternative papers, freelancing."

"What about the hit?"

"Levinson got it like you said. Cops found some weed and dissed the hate-crime angle, when his editor suggested it. No record that they ever questioned anybody from the ARM, since there was nothing at his place to prove he had a story in the works. From what I see here, one of the investigators thought it was a drug thing, while his partner claimed the weed was incidental to a burglary gone sour."

There was silence on the line while Bolan took that in, digesting it. "Okay," he said. "Maybe I'll give the guy a shot."

"What does he want?" Brognola asked.

"What else? Get even for his friend and file the story of a lifetime."

"I don't like the sound of that," Brognola said.

"Don't worry. We'll negotiate."

"Uh-huh." The big Fed didn't have to warn Bolan about exposing any secrets of the Farm. They'd both seen what could happen if its everyday facade was torn away, secrets and personnel exposed to enemies at large. The wounds from that traumatic episode had never fully healed.

They never would.

"I'll keep an eye on Jimmy Olsen," Bolan promised. "If he gets too squirrelly, you can always slap him in PC."

Protective custody raised problems of its own, Brognola knew, starting with the question of eventual release. It wasn't meant to take the place of life imprisonment without parole. Insuring silence was the snag. Better to recognize a problem early on, he thought, and snuff it out for good.

"We'll see," he answered noncommittally. "Where are you going next?"

"I haven't asked, yet," Bolan said. "No point, if the report came back thumbs-down."

"You'll keep me posted, though?"

"Sure thing."

"If you need transportation—"

"I know who to call. Stay frosty, eh?"

"You, too."

Brognola listened to the dial tone for a moment, then replaced the handset in its cradle. Bolan knew what he was doing. Always had. Brognola only hoped the wild card in the game wouldn't leave his friend with the dead man's hand.

10

"Gentlemen." Curt Walgren smiled around the word, scanning the faces ranged in front of him. "Warriors! Hail victory!"

They answered with a single voice, their right arms raised like rigid lances in salute. "Hail victory!"

"Sit, please."

The six brown-shirted soldiers settled onto metal folding chairs. Fluorescent ceiling lights reflected from their shaved scalps and their spit-shined boots. Each man was marked with scars, tattoos and psychic wounds that made him who he was. Together, they were soldiers of a higher cause.

"We stand," Walgren said, "at the brink of something great and terrible. Triumph or tragedy awaits us. I won't lie to you, my warriors. It could still go either way."

The soldiers shifted on their chairs, boots scuffing concrete. They were all better at fighting than at sitting still. To Walgren, the propensity for violence was their most endearing quality.

"You did a great job in Ohio," he declared. "The cash is more than welcome in our struggle against ZOG. Unfortunately, as you may have heard by now, we've suffered setbacks in the past two days."

The six waited. Whatever questions roiled inside their minds, they wouldn't speak unless directly questioned or invited to comment.

"Warriors, we have been subject to attack." That stiffened

spines and curled lips into snarls, as Walgren forged ahead. "Camp Yahweh was the first target, night before last. We suffered losses, both of lives and property. One raider was reported, though it's possible that others went unseen. He stole one of our vehicles and managed to escape despite pursuit. Commandant Grundy's efforts to identify the trespasser so far have not produced results."

One of the soldiers growled, a muffled sound, as if there was an angry dog in the next room. Walgren suspected it was Gellar, but it could've been Thompson or Fuchs.

"Last night," he told them, "while Commandant Hall was in the process of eliminating an informer, one or more invaders struck Camp Nordland. They removed the spy, killed seven loyal men and disappeared. Again, pursuit was fruitless. Now, we're under scrutiny from the police and ZOG, as never in our history before. We have a choice, warriors. We can surrender and disband, or mutate into a pathetic coffee klatsch society like the John Birchers, or we can retaliate in force and show the world what to expect from Aryans. Which will it be?"

Unleashed, the six men bolted to their feet, arms hoisted toward the ceiling as they bellowed out, "Hail victory! Hail victory!"

"In Yahweh's name," Walgren pronounced.

"Amen! Hail victory!"

"Be seated, please."

Reluctantly, they settled back into their chairs. All eyes were locked on Walgren's face, gleaming with zeal that bordered on insanity. "It's time to use the Thunderbolt again," he said.

On Walgren's left, Tom Chalmers clenched his fists so tightly that the knuckles cracked. Mike Connolly was grinning with a ravenous expression that explained, at least in part, his "Mad Dog" nickname.

"Our next target is not singled out for profit," Walgren said, "though ZOG owes much to us for its accumulated crime. We strike this time to teach our enemies a lesson. Let them learn the bitter taste of fear."

His soldiers fairly quivered in their seats, awaiting Walgren's signal for another round of chanting, but he let them wait. He wanted them on edge, keyed up, ready to fight.

Ready to kill.

"The day of victory is now within our grasp," Walgren said. "It is ours to win or lose. What we give up in numbers to the enemy, we can reclaim with our audacity, our courage, and our natural superiority. Yahweh is on our side and will assist us, but we have to do our part. He helps warriors who help themselves. Amen!"

"Amen!" came back at him from six taut throats.

"The target I've selected won't secure a victory outright," Walgren explained, "but it will warn our enemies that they are dealing with a force beyond their understanding or control. In fear lies weakness. When they learn to live in terror, then our enemies are one step from defeat."

The six soldiers in front of him were literally on the edges of their seats, hands clutching knees or clenched as fists atop their thighs. Walgren could see the thick veins pulsing in their necks and temples, marking each beat of the hearts he claimed as his.

These men would die for him upon command. They had already proved their willingness to kill.

"Before I brief you on the details of your mission, I want each of you to understand the risk involved, the trust I've placed in you, and the responsibility you carry. Chalmers!"

Bolting to his feet, the skinhead shouted, "Understood, sir!"

"Connolly?"

"Yes, sir!"

"Fuchs?"

"Loud and clear, sir!"

"Gellar?"

"Anytime, anywhere, sir!"

"Thompson?"

"Ready, sir!"

"Warren?"

"In Yahweh's name!"

That moved them all to another "Amen!" and Walgren left them standing as he turned to face an easel mounted just behind him. On the easel stood a map of the Midwest, pinned onto cardboard.

"Gentlemen," he told them, pointing, "this is where we strike next, in the holy war against our enemies."

The sudden burst of cheering made him smile.

11

The region known as "Deep East" Texas was an area where time, in some respects, stood still. Life had a slower pace than may be found in Houston, Dallas and Fort Worth. Ideas were slow to change, and some—particularly in regard to race and politics—appeared to have been carved in stone during the nineteenth century. Deep East Texas was the last part of the state to give up segregation, and its last known lynching was recorded in the spring of 1998.

It was the kind of place, Bolan thought, where a man like Neville Hoskins might feel very much at home. A place where others might protect him, watch his back and warn him if a stranger started asking questions, sniffing at his trail.

Coyle claimed that he could circumvent those risks, but Bolan wasn't absolutely sure.

Driving through Upshur County, keeping one eye on the rearview mirror for patrol cars, Bolan said, "I'm still not clear on how you know where Hoskins goes to ground."

"Research," his passenger replied. "I hear things, dig around for details, ask whatever I can get away with asking at the time. In this case, one of Hall's skinheads was talking about guns. Is that a shocker? Anyway, he mentioned hauling guns for Hoskins, trying to avoid the ATF. Said Nellie had a run-down farm in Texas, outside Cedar Springs, in someone else's name. He stashes weapons there and hides out when the heat's on."

The geography made sense to Bolan. In a pinch, Hoskins

could drive from Poplar Bluff, Missouri, to the Texas farm in three or four hours, depending on his speed. It also made a change from running to St. Louis, Little Rock, or Kansas City, where authorities were often more alert to fugitives. The good ol' boys in Deep East might not sympathize with all of the fanatical beliefs Hoskins espoused, but he would stand a better chance than in the city—any city—where customs and society were more in tune with the twenty-first century.

"You hear about the cop out here, a few years back, who beat one of his prisoners to death?" Coyle asked. "Black guy, of course. Some kind of farmer. Anyway, this cop was beating the hell out of the guy, in front of six or seven witnesses, when *bam!*—his blackjack falls apart. Cop looks around, grinning, and tells the witnesses, 'They sure don't make 'em like they used to,' and he goes to get a billy club, finishes the job. He's doing life now, but the locals never would've charged him if the SPLC hadn't tipped the media and filed a suit for wrongful death."

"SPLC?" Bolan inquired.

"Southern Poverty Law Center," Coyle explained. "They're based in Alabama, file all kinds of lawsuits against Nazis, Klansmen, racist cops. About ten years ago they put a whole Klan group out of business. Won a seven million dollar judgment in a murder case and forced the KKK to sell its headquarters." Coyle chuckled at the thought.

"They haven't sued the ARM, though?" Bolan asked.

"Not yet. With private groups, they only file when there's a pattern of criminal action dictated or clearly supported by recognized leaders. You remember Bob Mentzer?"

Bolan shook his head.

"Guy out in Utah, used to run White Aryan Revival from the backroom of his TV repair shop. He recruited lots of skinheads, stirred them up against minorities and turned them loose. One chapter in Las Vegas beat a guy to death with baseball bats supplied by one of Mentzer's so-called captains, and the SPLC took them on. A jury found that Mentzer not only directed and encouraged racial violence, but supplied the killers with their weapons. Next thing you know, he's bankrupt, blaming the whole thing on Jews."

Another chuckle, though the subject matter didn't seem that humorous to Bolan. "Eleven miles to Cedar Springs," he said, reading a highway sign.

"Still daylight," Coyle observed. "You want to stop somewhere?"

"We might as well."

The drive from Taos had consumed eleven hours and change, but there was light left in the day, as Coyle observed. Bolan would've preferred a daytime recon of his target, but he knew how rural folk sometimes reacted to strange men and vehicles. He'd wait for sundown, scout the place in darkness, and delay the probe until another night if any special gear was needed.

"If you're looking for motels," Coyle said, "I would suggest two rooms. Out here, the clerk might drop a dime to Deputy Dawg."

Or someone else, Bolan thought.

There was no clear reason to suspect the ARM had infiltrated law enforcement, but it wouldn't be the first time an extremist group picked up recruits among frustrated cops or those with a malicious mean streak. Bolan planned to take no chances, either way. "We'll get something to eat," he said. "Kill time some other way."

"Suits me. But what about tonight?" Coyle asked.

"You're coming with me," Bolan said. It was a choice he'd made reluctantly, considering that he could ill afford to leave the journalist alone, unsupervised, while he went seeking Hoskins.

"Really?" Coyle sounded excited, almost childlike.

"Don't make me regret it," Bolan said.

"I won't!"

Frowning, Bolan signaled for his exit.

NIGHTS WERE THE WORST for Neville Hoskins. He didn't like the noises that continued all night long, throughout the old farmhouse. Whether it was the wind outside, a branch scraping on windowpanes, or rodents scuttling in the walls, each sound increased his personal anxiety.

I'm safe, he told himself. Was that the hundredth or the thousandth time he'd tried to calm his jangling nerves by simple reason? Either way, it wasn't working.

Hoskins knew he should be safe in Texas, but that didn't mean he *was*. At least two dozen ARM members had seen the farm, and Yahweh only knew how many others they had told, in turn. The thought made Hoskins want to pack and flee again, but where else could he go? If cops and Feds were after him, they'd have staked out his sister's place in Baton Rouge.

Too bad. The old bitch never liked him, anyway.

"I'm safe," he said aloud, surprised at how his voice fell flat and dead into the musty sitting room. He had the curtains drawn. One lamp illuminated the smallish house. He paid the power bills, reluctantly, because the well's pump was electric and he needed water when he visited the farm, approximately once per month. He also needed power for the workshop, where he tinkered with assorted weapons and explosives during his retreats.

There'd been no work so far, on this trip. Hoskins was in hiding, plain and simple, since the raid on Camp Yahweh and the attack that followed one day later, in New Mexico. A cheap television kept him informed of national and world events, reminding Hoskins that there'd been no breaks yet, in the case. His picture hadn't shown up on the tube with "WANTED" underneath it, but that didn't mean he wasn't being hunted. ZOG's agents were ruthless, and they didn't always carry out their missions in the public eye.

"I'm ready for them," Hoskins told the empty room.

Arrayed in front of him, across a low-slung coffee table,

were the gunsmith's weapons of choice. To his left lay a Russian AKS, the folding-stock version of the vintage AK-47, loaded with a curved banana clip. Beside the rifle, he had placed a 12-gauge Ithaca 37 shotgun, with an extended 8-round magazine. Next to the shotgun lay a matching pair of Colt M-1911 A-1 semiauto pistols, the classic .45-caliber side arms carried by U.S. military personnel from World War I through the Vietnam era. The last piece on the table was a twelve-inch Bowie knife, but if it came to blade work, Hoskins figured he was screwed.

Too close, too little and too late.

Waiting made Hoskins nervous, always had. He'd been a jumpy child who grew into a restless man, only relaxed when he was fiddling with some weapon, preferably with a six-pack close at hand. He'd brought no alcohol along this time, however, since the crisis called for clear, cool thinking.

He was clear, all right—but far from cool.

A sound outside brought Hoskins to his feet, snatching the AKS. Was that a footstep in the yard outside? Someone advancing on the house?

He set the rifle down, picked up the shotgun, then reversed his choice again. Buckshot was better if he didn't have a chance to aim, but shooting through the walls required more power, and projectiles with full-metal jackets.

Hoskins wondered whether he should go and have a look around, outside. He hated the idea, but waiting in the house for someone to surprise him—or to set the place on fire—was foolish.

"Nothing there," he muttered. "Why not go see?"

Hoskins set down the rifle, tucked the twin Colt .45s into his belt, butts facing forward, then retrieved the AKS once more. He jacked a round into the rifle's chamber, taking comfort from the loud metallic noise it made.

Better.

He killed the lamp and moved through darkness toward the

exit, thankful that the room held little furniture. An obstacle course was the last thing he needed right now. He moved through the kitchen by moonlight, unlocked the back door and stepped into the night.

Crickets silenced their chirping as Hoskins emerged from the house. Something whirred overhead, maybe bats, but his mind focused closer to Earth. He was looking for prowlers, not fairies. If—

There!

Something dark and man-sized broke from cover, near the barn, and sprinted toward a nearby shed. Yelping in surprise, Hoskins leveled his rifle and squeezed off a burst of automatic fire.

BOLAN WAS ON THE FAR SIDE of the farmhouse when the shooting started. He assumed that Coyle somehow had managed to reveal himself, despite strict warnings to remain hidden behind the barn until he heard Bolan call his name.

The Executioner was checking windows when the unmistakable report of a Kalashnikov distracted him. He circled toward the west side of the house with cautious strides, ducking below each window that he passed. They had assumed Hoskins would be alone, but it was unconfirmed. Another shooter could be waiting in the house, ready to fire the moment a target presented itself.

He reached the southwest corner of the house unchallenged, peered around it and observed a chunky gunman running toward the barn. Bolan glanced toward the porch, saw nothing to suggest another watcher there, and took a chance by moving in pursuit.

He could've dropped the hunter easily, at that range, but he took for granted that the man was Neville Hoskins. Killing him before they had a chance to talk would make the probe a waste of time, which Bolan couldn't easily afford. If Coyle had placed himself at risk—which seemed to be the case, despite his orders—Bolan meant to take advantage of the lapse which had, if nothing else, lured Hoskins from the house.

It was a thirty-yard run to the barn, the dark house behind him, and with each step Bolan expected a blaze of gunfire at his back that never came. Coyle had believed Hoskins would be alone, and now it seemed that he'd been right.

Why couldn't he stay put as ordered, without blundering around and complicating matters? Bolan guessed it was the journalist's instinct for seeking information—or for finding trouble, in this case. It wouldn't please him if the ARM's gunsmith shot Coyle before he had a chance to intervene, but neither would the fault be Bolan's.

They had covered Coyle's role in the probe—a strictly silent, stationary one—and Coyle had readily agreed to follow Bolan's rules. It came as no great shock that Coyle betrayed that trust, and so it would be no great cause for mourning if he paid the price.

What difference did another ghost make, when the Executioner already trailed so many in his wake?

Bolan couldn't see Coyle in the darkness ahead, but he assumed that Hoskins had to be trailing and firing at something. If not, then a delusion would've served him well, drawing the gunsmith from his house into the open.

Closer.

Bolan reached a corner of the barn, while Hoskins jogged on past it, circling toward a nearby shed. The warrior grimaced when his prey squeezed off another burst, relaxing only slightly when no cry rang out in answer.

If the bullets found him, Coyle might have no chance to scream. He could be dead already, twitching in the farmyard dust, while Bolan crept along behind his killer.

But if so, the harm was done. Killing the only source left on his list wouldn't help Bolan carry out his mission. He could always deal with Nellie Hoskins afterward, once he had spilled his guts.

Bolan advanced, holding the Colt Commando braced against his shoulder, sighting down its barrel at his target, with his index finger on the trigger. It would only take a gentle squeeze to finish Hoskins or cut his legs from under him and leave him squalling on the ground.

Trick shots were risky, though. Intent wasn't required to score a kill. Even a well-aimed bullet, simply meant to wing a mark, could snip an artery and bleed the target dry in no time. It would be better, if he could, to take Hoskins without resort to deadly force.

Assuming that was possible.

Hoskins had nearly reached the corner of the shed. Another step or two would take him out of Bolan's sight and make pursuit more hazardous. Advancing with no enemy in view, he might be ambushed. Was it possible that Hoskins knew he had been followed? That his acting skills were strong enough to let him inch around the shed, oblivious to danger on his flank, before he turned to catch the hunter by surprise?

Doubtful. But Bolan didn't want to take that chance.

Moving as quickly as he could, with long silent strides, he closed the gap between himself and Hoskins. They were barely fifteen feet apart as Hoskins took a deep breath, hunched his shoulders and prepared to turn the corner of the shed.

Bolan rushed forward at the final instant, carbine raised and drove its butt with crushing force into the point behind one of the Nazi gunsmith's ears. Without a word, Hoskins collapsed into a heap.

Bolan stood over Hoskins for a moment, then called out, "It's finished, Coyle. I've got him. If you're still alive, get over here!"

"I CALL THAT REAL CONCERN," Coyle muttered, as the two of them half dragged, half carried Hoskins toward the house.

"You're wasting breath," Bolan replied.

"At least I'm breathing, pal. As if you care."

"You had instructions. You ignored them. Stupid choices have a price."

"Oh, now I'm stupid?"

"Breaking cover against orders. If the shoe fits—"

"I wanted a piece of the action, all right?"

"And you got it. Now focus!"

Hoskins was deadweight in their hands as they approached the broad front porch, but Bolan veered off toward the south side of the house.

"Hey, why don't we—"

"He came out through the kitchen," Bolan interrupted. "There's an open door."

By the time they reached the kitchen door, Coyle's shoulders ached, his biceps burned, and he felt a disturbing tingle in his fingers. "Jeez," he said. "I thought I was in shape."

Bolan, sounding fit and rested, said, "It's not much farther."

In the kitchen, they dumped Hoskins on the floor, then found a light switch to illuminate the place. After a glance around, Coyle felt the grumbling in his stomach rapidly subside.

"Man, talk about your greasy spoon."

"We didn't come to eat. Let's put him in a chair."

They raised Hoskins one more time, into a chair that bore his weight reluctantly. Bolan found duct tape in a drawer and made strategic applications to the captive's wrists and ankles, finishing with three wide loops around the midsection that bound Hoskins into his chair. Throughout the binding, there was no sign of life.

"Did you kill him?" Coyle asked.

"No. He's breathing."

Bolan found a dirty glass, filled it with water from the kitchen tap and threw the water in their captive's face. It worked, like in the movies, Hoskins sputtering and blinking as he struggled back to consciousness. The part most movies *didn't* show was the explosive vomiting that came with waking, after being knocked out cold.

"Feel better now?" Bolan asked.

Hoskins stared at each of them in turn, wincing as if the light in the kitchen hurt his eyes. "I knew you pricks was comin'," Hoskins said.

"You're psychic?" Bolan prodded him. "Why don't you tell us why we're here?"

"To kill me, Jew boy. Why'n hell else would you come?"

"You think I'm Jewish?" Bolan asked.

"Or else ZOG bought your rotten soul. It's all the same to me. Scumbags, the both of you."

"So tell me something," Bolan said. "Why are you still alive?"

Hoskins had no quick answer for that. He shrugged within the limits of his duct tape corset, glowering at each of them.

"I'll help you out," Bolan said. "You have certain information that I need. I'll ask the questions. You can answer them or not, depending on how much you want to stay alive and in one piece."

"Bullshit!" Hoskins spit. "You'll get nothin' outta me."

"Oh, I'll get something out of you," Bolan replied. "It may be information, maybe flesh and blood. But something, never fear."

"You may as well get started, then," Hoskins said.

"Suit yourself."

The Executioner moved through the kitchen. He filled a pan, which he placed on the stove to boil. From drawers and counters he retrieved three knives of different lengths, a corkscrew, mallet and a meat cleaver. He placed those in a tidy lineup on the kitchen table, Hoskins watching closely as he set each item in its place.

"All right, here's how it works," Bolan said. "When I ask a question, you have ten seconds to answer. If you don't, or if I think you're lying, then I claim a pound of flesh and ask again. You follow me?"

"I won't say nothin'."

"Fair enough. I figure you're about 240, give or take. That can't be healthy. Maybe we can slim you down. First question—tell me everything you know about the thunderbolt."

Hoskins blinked rapidly, apparently surprised, then bit his

lip and shook his head. Bolan stood waiting, counting seconds on his watch until the prisoner ran out of time.

"Strike one," the inquisitor said. He turned and took a butcher knife from the array of tools, held up its foot-long blade to catch the light. "So, that's a pound you owe me, Nellie. I'll try not to hit an artery."

Bolan stood over Hoskins, ripped the left sleeve of his shirt free at the shoulder, pulled it down and seized a pinch of fatty flesh with his fingers. Hoskins had begun to hyperventilate, then screamed at his first contact with the blade, before it broke his skin.

"All right! I'll talk! Don't cut me, Jesus!"

"Do you want me to repeat the question?"

"No! The Thunderbolt! I seen it! Sure I did!"

Coyle blinked, surprised. Was Hoskins lying out of fear, or did the supergun really exist?

"Where did you see it?" Bolan asked.

"Right here. They brung it to me, let me look it over, like. Make sure it works and all."

"Describe it for me."

Hoskins looked pathetic with tears streaming down his florid, unshaved face. "Well, it's about the same size as a .50-caliber," he replied. "Maybe a little heavier. It's single-shot, though, kinda like the old recoilless rifles. Got a laser sight with batteries, so not a thing's wasted but the target."

"What about the ammunition?" Bolan urged.

"Looks like your basic twenty millimeter, but the bullet's somethin' else. It's got a core like phosphorus, but differ'nt. Walgren didn't tell me what it was. I asked him could he leave me one or two to play with, but he wouldn't do it."

"How's it work?" Bolan asked.

"Somethin' sparks on impact, and it shoots this stream of white-hot metal straight through damn near anything. We didn't test it on titanium, of course, but Kevlar, steel, concrete. You name it."

"Tell me where to find it, and we're finished here."

"I'm suppose to meet a bunch of 'em tomorrow," Hoskins said. "Give it another check before some mission they got goin'."

"When and where?"

"Place up north of Tulsa, in the Cookson Hills. I told 'em I'd be there about sundown."

"We'll need directions."

Hoskins nodded, started naming towns, describing landmarks. Bolan didn't write it down, but Coyle suspected that he hadn't missed a thing.

"WHY DIDN'T YOU KILL HIM?" Coyle demanded, when they got back on the road.

"We left him tied up in the house. My friends will take care of him," Bolan said.

"Right. Okay." Coyle brooded for a mile or so, then asked, "Who *are* you, really? I mean, cops don't act like this."

"I never claimed to be a cop."

"Answer the question, will you?"

"No."

"That's it? Just, 'No'?"

"That's it."

"I guess the Constitution just went out the window, huh? The Fifth Amendment? How about the First? If there's some kind of covert operation killing people in this country without due process of law, the people have a right to know!"

"Since when do you speak for the people?" Bolan challenged. "Who appointed you as the collective conscience?"

"There's no appointment necessary," Coyle replied. "In case you missed that day in civics class, we're guaranteed a *free* press in this country."

"And that's you? What makes you think the people even want to know what's happening?" Bolan asked.

"Excuse me?"

"Think about it. How many would rather watch Reality TV than C-SPAN? Who protests corruption scandals in the government? Who demonstrates when stem-cell research gets the ax? Who even thinks about the risk of global warming?"

"So you're saying—"

"What I'm saying," Bolan cut him short, "is that some things are done because they *must* be. Some are chosen to perform because they can. And some news doesn't make the cut because the people couldn't handle it."

"So, you're a fan of government by secrecy?"

"This isn't government," Bolan replied. "I'm taking out the trash."

"And I'm supposed to help you?"

"That's a fine selective memory you've got there. Whose idea was it, again, for you to tag along?"

"I didn't know—"

"Well, now you do," Bolan said. "And you're either on the team, or I can drop you off with friends who'll keep you safe and sound until the smoke clears."

"What about my story?"

"There you have it. Altruism in a nutshell."

Two miles later, Coyle inquired, "So, what's up next?"

"The Cookson Hills," Bolan replied. "A little slice of history."

12

The Cookson Hills, in northeastern Oklahoma, have served as a refuge for bandits and outcasts since the nineteenth century. Bill Doolin's gang, the Dalton brothers and a host of others hid out there in the decades following the Civil War, outwitting Pinkerton detectives and U.S. marshals alike. In the 1930s, the Cooksons sheltered fugitives such as Bonnie and Clyde, the Barker-Karpis gang, and "Pretty Boy" Floyd. To this day, the area remains a hotbed of illicit moonshine stills and cash crops cultivated to go up in smoke.

Geography is not the only benefit for outlaws in the Cookson Hills. The locals, often reared in poverty, neglected or abused by state and federal agencies, have often welcomed rebels who waged war against railroads and banks, sometimes against the government itself. If Missouri was once dubbed the "Mother of Bandits," then the Cookson Hills of Oklahoma were a kind of home-away-from-home.

Bolan knew that much history, at least, as he approached their destination. He was looking for a place outside Bluejacket, in Craig County, following directions from a dead man. Coyle had given up on asking "Are we there yet?" after Bolan pinned him with a glare that could've curdled milk, and they had covered ground in silence for the past three-quarters of an hour.

Coyle broke the silence first, pointing ahead. "The Mail Pouch barn," he said.

"I see it."

It was next to last on Bolan's list of landmarks, but it wasn't hard to find. Barn art was rare, these days, but walls and roofs across the country had once boasted giant ads for Mail Pouch chewing tobacco. It was a good deal all around: hard-luck farmers got their barns painted free of charge by professionals, while the company scored low-cost advertising along highways throughout the nation. Most of the signs were weathered down to shadows of their former glory. Bolan couldn't honestly recall the last time he had seen a Mail Pouch sign so lovingly maintained.

"Next right," Coyle said.

"I'm on it."

It got tricky once they passed the Mail Pouch barn. Hoskins was scheduled for a meeting with his cronies from the ARM at sundown, which meant Bolan had to find *and* scout his target in broad daylight. If he waited any longer, giving Walgren's men a chance to stew about their tardy comrade, maybe try to reach the gunsmith on his cell phone, he could lose his targets and the Thunderbolt as well.

The name was stuck in Bolan's mind. He didn't buy the Aryan mythology behind it, but it worked as well as any other label for his purposes. If it was close enough to grab, he meant to have it.

After that...

He turned off the state highway, traveling northwest along a two-lane country road. Corn on one side, withered to a khaki shade behind a barbed-wire fence; trees on the other, stout and strong, but changing leaves ahead of time in testimony to a dearth of rainfall. Nature had its way of balancing the scales. Unfortunately, it had never worked with humankind.

Bolan was watching for the last landmark. He saw it on the left, marked it as Coyle said, "Graveyard up ahead."

"Got it."

Two hundred yards beyond the rural cemetery, Bolan passed the entrance to a private road, shadowed by trees on either side.

There was a chain across the road, sagging from fence posts, with a sign that read: TRESPASSERS WILL BE SHOT. SURVIVORS WILL BE SHOT AGAIN.

"They aren't even original," Coyle said. "Rockwell once had a sign like that at headquarters, in Arlington."

"If all else fails," Bolan replied, "I'll slap them with a plagiarism charge."

"You're keeping me in stitches over here," Coyle said.

"We aim to please."

"Uh-huh. So what's the plan, for real?"

"Find someplace we can stash the car," Bolan said. "Then go back on foot and have a look around, while there's still time."

"In daylight?"

"We don't know how long they'll wait for Hoskins after sunset. If it spooks them, missing him, they may take off abruptly. And if that happens, I don't want to be sitting in the car, a mile away."

"You'd try to stop them?"

"Why else am I here?"

"I'm still working on that," the journalist replied. "A man of mystery, a law unto himself, casing a Nazi secret weapon all over the map. I still can't get a handle on who's picking up the tab or why they want this supergun."

"I'm glad to hear it," Bolan said.

"But I'm not giving up."

"Of course not."

Some three-quarters of a mile beyond the chained road, Bolan found another barn. This one had fallen into massive disrepair, with yards of shingles missing from the swaybacked roof, walls leaning inward, overgrown by weeds and climbing vines. The double door that once admitted men and livestock was a gaping hole, like the entrance to a cave.

"Looks like a fair garage," Bolan said.

"What? You'd park in there?"

"Why not?"

He pulled off-road, slowing across a narrow strip of grass and wildflowers, braking when they were well inside the barn. There was no way to hide his tire tracks in the grass, but passersby would probably ignore them, if they weren't alert to signs of trespass.

Stepping from the car in semidarkness, the Executioner saw a black-and-white king snake vanish between two rotten slats of the north wall. It reassured him that they'd find no rattlers in the barn. Safe footing for the first step of his probe, at least. But after that, it would be danger all the way.

"We doing this, or what?" Coyle asked.

"We're doing it," Bolan replied. "But if you screw it up this time, you're on your own."

"How MUCH LONGER until sundown?" Ernie Fuchs inquired.

"We've got three windows in the fuckin' room," Mike Connolly replied. "When it gets dark, you'll know it."

Tom Chalmers and Ed Warren—"Blitz" and "War Child"—laughed at that. Fuchs thought of telling Connolly to screw himself, but that was risky. There were reasons for his "Mad Dog" nickname, chief among them an explosive temper that was absolutely unpredictable. Fuchs might've relished the encounter, under other circumstances, but the mission took priority.

For now.

"Six-thirty-seven," said Jake Thompson, known as "Doom" within the ARM. "Sundown. Six-thirty-seven."

"Shit, you sound like Rain Man," Connolly retorted.

"Fuck you, Doggy."

There was silence in the farmhouse parlor for a moment, until Connolly slumped back into the sagging couch and said, "Whatever, man."

Roy Gellar sat beside the nearest window, covering the long driveway. "Now that we took the chain down, he should be here anytime."

"Old Nellie," Chalmers said. "You think he's gay?"

"I never thought about it," Gellar said. His fingers idly traced the long scar on one cheek that made them call him "Razor."

"That'd be a fuckin' joke," Connolly said. "A faggot handling the arsenal."

"The man knows guns, and Walgren checked him out," Gellar replied. "You want to ask him when he gets here, wait till *after* he's done messing with the Thunderbolt."

"Me ask him?" Chalmers challenged. "Why the hell would I do that?"

"It's preying on your mind," Gellar said. "Must be something makes you think about it."

"Hey, man—"

"He's got you there, Blitz," Connolly chimed in. "You in the mood for fudge, or what?"

"You fuckin' guys."

The laughter went around, one circuit of the musty room, then died. All six of them were tired of waiting. Fuchs could see it on the faces of the others, etched in lines around their mouths and eyes. If Hoskins didn't show up soon...

"Somebody oughta check the van," Warren said.

"Why?" Gellar asked.

"Just in case."

"In case of what?"

"Prowlers or somethin'."

"Jesus. Prowlers."

"Hey, you never know, with what's been going on."

"He's right," Fuchs said. "That's funny shit."

"What's funny, Gasser?" Warren asked. "We lost a dozen men the past two days."

"Not ha-ha funny," Fuchs explained. *"Weird* funny. Like we've never had that kinda trouble, now it's everywhere."

"Don't get your panties in a twist," Connolly said, sneering. "We still got—"

"Smoke!" Gellar cried out. "The fuckin' barn's on fire!"

Fuchs rose and took his M-1 carbine with him, moving toward the window first, while others rushed the door.

"Wait up!" Gellar snapped. "This could be a trap. Blitz, Doom and Mad Dog, go out through the back and circle around. Head for the barn. Waste anybody you don't recognize."

Those three were moving when he added, "War Child, come with me to check the van, before we hit the barn. Gasser, stay here and cover us."

"But I—"

"Just do it!"

Secretly, Fuchs was relieved. He yearned for action against ZOG, but this was something else. Some spooky shit was going down, and he'd be happy to sit back, waiting for targets to reveal themselves.

More smoke was drifting from the barn now, misty white. That told him it was wood smoke, even though he couldn't smell it. With a barn that old, Fuchs knew it wouldn't take much to ignite the dried-out lumber or any remnants of hay still inside. A simple spark would do it.

But what struck the spark?

Make that *who*.

The farm was old, abandoned and dilapidated, but its buildings had survived the best part of a century without bursting into flame from spontaneous combustion. Fuchs assumed there was a human hand at work behind the smoke that twined and thickened in the air outside.

But whose?

He clutched the shotgun to his chest and scanned the yard with eager eyes. Gellar and Warren were advancing toward the van, their weapons primed and ready. While they focused mainly on the barn, both men were shooting glances all around them, watching out for unseen enemies.

Fuchs almost missed it when a stranger peered around the northwest corner of the barn. His face was there and gone, drawn back almost before the image registered. Fuchs jerked the window open, needing all his strength to get it halfway up, then braced his weapon on the sill.

"There's someone over by the barn!" he called to Gellar and Warren. "The corner nearest you!"

Just then, the face appeared once more, and Fuchs triggered a blast to take the stranger down.

RANDY COYLE was crouched behind an oak tree, studying the house and wishing that he had a camera, when three skinheads with rifles exited the back door and began to move around to the front. Coyle had no way of warning Cooper, but he couldn't bring himself to simply sit and watch the trap closing around his strange companion.

Whispering a curse, he rose and started moving through the trees, keeping well out of sight as he jogged parallel to the ARM gunmen. After several strides, he noted something in the air, a tangy smell that sense and memory identified as wood smoke.

Cooper!

The big man had warned that he'd planned some kind of a diversion, but no details were forthcoming. At the time, Coyle had supposed that his companion wasn't sure exactly what he'd do to lure the skinheads from their hidey-hole. Now, as he paused, scanning the yard, Coyle saw smoke drifting from the barn, perhaps a hundred feet north of the house.

Cooper had set that fire to draw his adversaries out, and they were coming for him. Some of them, at least. How many still remained inside the house was anybody's guess, and Coyle had barely formed that thought when two men suddenly appeared, leaving the front porch, moving toward two vehicles parked in the yard. One was a Ford sedan; the other was an old blue van.

A van.

There would be room inside it for the weapon Cooper called the Thunderbolt, and probably some to spare. Could it be there, almost within their reach? Coyle wondered.

A gunshot echoed from the house, and Coyle saw dust fly

as shotgun pellets struck a corner of the barn. He couldn't see
the shooter's target from that angle, but he hoped they hadn't
nailed Cooper already.

If they killed him, Coyle would be alone, unarmed.

What could he do, against those odds?

He had asked Cooper for a weapon and had been refused.
The answer came as no surprise to Coyle, and it did no good
to complain that he was simply interested in self-defense.
Cooper's reply—"Stay with the car"—had fallen on deaf ears.

Now, here he was, unarmed and watching helplessly while
two more skinheads started firing toward the barn. Coyle
couldn't see what they were shooting at, but it could only be
Matt Cooper. No return fire issued from the shadows over
there, and Coyle was worried that his guardian-companion
might've been cut down, might be dying as he stood trembling
in the dark.

What could he do about it?

Something.

Acting on impulse, he leaped from cover, waving both arms
overhead and shouted at the skinhead shooters, "Hey, you Nazi
bastards! Over here!"

Coyle waited for the first of them to turn, then spun and
raced into the woods, ducking and dodging as he ran. A sputtering of gunfire answered, bullets chasing him like some fierce
species of nocturnal hornet, buzzing through the night, some
of them slapping into tree trunks.

Stupid! Coyle chastised himself. Just fucking stupid!

Were they chasing him? Coyle couldn't tell, and he was ter-
rified to stop and check, for fear the slightest break in his wild
sprint might give a sniper time to draw a bead and cut him
down. It seemed, though, that the gunfire, while increased in
volume, was *receding* as he ran.

That made no sense to Coyle and brought him to a lurching
halt, gasping for air. Against his body's ravenous demand for
oxygen, he caught a breath and held it, listening. In place of

GET FREE BOOKS and a FREE GIFT WHEN YOU PLAY THE...

Lucky 7

SLOT MACHINE GAME!

Just scratch off the silver box with a coin. Then check below to see the gifts you get!

YES!
I have scratched off the silver box. Please send me the 2 free Gold Eagle® books and gift for which I qualify. I understand I am under no obligation to purchase any books, as explained on the back of this card.

366 ADL EEZ3   **166 ADL EEZR**

FIRST NAME

LAST NAME

ADDRESS

APT.#

CITY

STATE/PROV.

ZIP/POSTAL CODE

7	7	7	**Worth TWO FREE BOOKS** plus a **BONUS** Mystery Gift!
🍒	🍒	🍒	**Worth TWO FREE BOOKS!**
♣	♣	♣	**Worth ONE FREE BOOK!**
🔔	🔔	🍒	**TRY AGAIN!**

(GE-L7-06)

DETACH AND MAIL CARD TODAY!

The Gold Eagle Reader Service™ — Here's how it works:

Accepting your 2 free books and mystery gift places you under no obligation to buy anything. You may keep the books and gift and return the shipping statement marked "cancel." If you do not cancel, about a month later we'll send you 6 additional books and bill you just $29.94* — that's a savings of over 10% off the cover price of all 6 books! And there's no extra charge for shipping! You may cancel at any time, but if you choose to continue, every other month we'll send you 6 more books, which you may either purchase at the discount price or return to us and cancel your subscription.

*Terms and prices subject to change without notice. Sales tax applicable in N.Y. Canadian residents will be charged applicable provincial taxes and GST. Credit or debit balances in a customer's account(s) may be offset by any other outstanding balance owed by or to the customer.

If offer card is missing write to: Gold Eagle Reader Service, 3010 Walden Ave., P.O. Box 1867, Buffalo NY 14240-186

NO POSTAGE
NECESSARY
IF MAILED
IN THE
UNITED STATES

BUSINESS REPLY MAIL
FIRST-CLASS MAIL   PERMIT NO. 717-003   BUFFALO, NY

POSTAGE WILL BE PAID BY ADDRESSEE

GOLD EAGLE READER SERVICE
3010 WALDEN AVE
PO BOX 1867
BUFFALO NY 14240-9952

the pursuit sounds he'd expected, there was only shooting, apparently still emanating from the farmyard.

Cooper!

Cursing bitterly, Coyle turned back toward the killing ground. His mind and gut agreed that he should run and keep on running, until he was well away from anyone inclined to kill him, but some other instinct drew him back to the farmhouse. It might've been the story, though he wasn't sure there'd ever be one—particularly if he stopped a bullet taking stupid chances in a combat zone.

What else, then?

Coyle had no time left to think about it as he neared the rundown homestead. Peering through the trees, he saw four skinheads piling into the old van, one of them in the driver's seat and revving up the engine. His companions laid down cover fire, strafing the yard and barn. Two others were on foot and racing toward the Ford sedan.

They'll get away! Coyle thought, and cursing, scoured the ground around his feet for anything that might serve as a weapon. Scooping up a stone the size of a baseball, Coyle stepped from cover, cocked his arm and hurled it toward the stragglers with all his might.

THE SHOOTERS WEREN'T half bad. Bolan gave credit to his enemies, where it was due, but credit didn't translate into sympathy. They'd stalled him, pinned him down and made him scuttle like a mouse dodging a hungry owl, but they had not escaped.

Not yet.

He fired a short burst at the van, as it began to move, and saw his 5.56 mm bullets scar the paint along its starboard flank. That wouldn't slow them down, but if the slugs drilled through, they might wound one of the skinheads or even damage their cargo.

Bolan had no doubt that the Thunderbolt was in that van, accelerating out of range as he emerged from cover near the barn. Two more skinheads remained, rushing to catch their ride and firing random shots around the farmyard as they ran. His car, by contrast, was three-quarters of a mile away, parked in a barn.

He needed wheels, and there was only one set available. Bolan shouldered his weapon, sighting on the nearest target, and he was already taking up the trigger slack when something strange happened downrange.

His target staggered, nearly fell, and clutched one cheek, blood streaming through his fingers. As the skinhead swiveled to identify his enemy, Bolan saw Randy Coyle standing exposed, near the tree line, shaking his fist.

"How's that, you prick?" Coyle shouted. "I pitched varsity for two straight years!"

The battered skinhead didn't seem to care about Coyle's record as an athlete. Kicking at the stone, where it had fallen near his feet, he raised a shotgun to his shoulder, microseconds from a kill.

The Colt Commando stuttered, spitting out a 3-round burst that caught the skinhead by surprise and lifted him on tiptoe, punched him sideways, took him down. The dying man fired the shotgun anyway, but it was wasted on the dirt ten feet in front of him, raising a cloud of dust that drifted back to settle on the shooter's lifeless face.

That left one, on the far side of the Ford, and he already had the driver's door open. He wasn't invisible, but Bolan pictured him inside the car, leaning across the seat, fumbling to turn the key. How long to get it rolling and be out of there, leaving the Executioner to wonder where his prey had gone this time?

Bolan moved forward, cut the gap by half, then knelt and fired two quick shots through the passenger door. Penetration was no problem, with the thin sheet metal used on cars, but he could only wonder about hits unless his target rose to fight or flee.

Nothing.

He fired a third shot, angling for a through-and-through. In one door, out the other. If the skinhead *was* inside the car, or even crouching by the open driver's door to reach beneath the dashboard—

"Over here!" Coyle shouted from the sidelines. "I can see him! Hey, you skinhead prick!"

A wiser man would've ignored him, but wisdom and "Master Race" pipe dreams had nothing in common. The skinhead stood up, aimed a carbine at Coyle and squeezed off two quick shots.

Bolan nailed him before he could trigger a third, firing straight through the Ford's open window this time. A single bullet did the job, drilling his chest from side to side and mangling vital organs as it passed. Coyle ran across the farmyard, seemingly unhurt, and snatched the carbine from his fallen enemy.

"I may need this," he said, as Bolan reached the Ford.

"Try not to shoot yourself—or me," Bolan replied.

"No sweat. I trained on these when I joined up." Coyle stared after the taillights of the rapidly retreating van. "So, are we going after them, or what?"

Bolan leaned through the open driver's door and saw the key in place. "As soon as you get in the car," he said.

The Ford responded to his touch, and Bolan gunned it from a standing start. Momentum slammed Coyle's door before he had a chance to close it, pressing both men back into their seats. The tires spit dirt and gravel as they peeled out of the farmyard, barreling along the driveway with its overhanging arch of trees.

"I think we're looking at the supergun right there," Coyle chattered, pointing through their dusty windshield at the van. "You think so, too?"

"It's worth a look," Bolan replied.

He concentrated on the target and the risk. Four gunmen in the van, all packing small arms, and perhaps a little something extra they could trot out in emergencies. Bolan had come to find the Thunderbolt, and while he hadn't glimpsed it yet, he shared Coyle's feeling that they had to be close. The van and hasty flight all tallied with the information Hoskins had provided.

All they had to do was nail it down.

And not get killed.

One of the skinheads leaned out of a right-hand window, brandishing a pistol, and fired three quick shots in Bolan's general direction. None of them came within six feet of the Ford, but the soldier took no chances, drifting far enough leftward to block the shooter's view.

Before Bolan could stop him, Coyle had thrust his borrowed carbine out the window and returned fire, sending half a dozen shots after the van. One of them actually hit the square back door, low down, and knocked a shiny divot in the paint.

Bolan took one hand off the wheel, snagged Coyle's collar and dragged him back inside. "No firing, understand?"

"But they—"

"Don't make me drop you here."

"Jesus, okay! I hit 'em, though!"

"Sit back and put the safety on, right now."

Coyle did as he was told, with undisguised bad humor. He was in a fighting mood, keyed up for action, but he was an amateur. Their mission—Bolan's mission—went beyond stopping the van and riddling it with bullets.

He was looking for the Thunderbolt, intent on taking it intact, if possible. If not, he needed to make sure that its destruction was complete.

No second shot at Armageddon for the ARM.

And once they had the weapon...

"What the hell?"

Bolan had seen the van's back door swing open just before Coyle spoke. He wasn't close enough, yet, for his high beams to illuminate the other vehicle's interior, but Bolan didn't have to guess why someone in the van had sprung the door.

"Stay down!" he ordered, as a muzzle-flash winked at them from the dark cave of the van. Another joined it, as the first slug chipped their windshield, high on Bolan's side.

He swerved the car, fishtailing, back and forth across the driveway. In the van, two gunners were intent on peppering the Ford until it stalled or rolled.

"Can I shoot now?" Coyle asked.

"Feel free."

He opened up with gusto, firing half a magazine while Bolan drove his swerving zigzag course. "Hey, man," Coyle said, "can't you drive straight?"

"Not if you want to live."

"Jerking around this way, I can't—"

A different kind of muzzle-flash blossomed inside the van. Larger, brighter. Coyle glimpsed it as well, and shouted, "Whoa!" before a sizzling bolt of *something* carved a scar across the Ford's broad hood.

"Mother of God!" Coyle shouted.

"Pray later!" Bolan snapped. "Shoot now!"

Coyle nodded jerkily and thrust his carbine back into the slipstream of the night, squeezing the semiauto weapon's trigger spastically. Beside him, Bolan drove one-handed, palming his Beretta 93-R for left-handed shooting from the driver's window. If he couldn't stop the shooters soon—

Another red-orange muzzle-flash erupted from the van. Bolan tried to anticipate the shot, cranking the wheel hard left, but with the gun itself invisible he couldn't estimate its point of aim with anything resembling accuracy.

They were swerving when the round seared through the Ford's thick radiator, burned across or through the engine block and exited the dashboard, taking out the radio and tape deck in a cloud of smoke and sparks. Bolan stood hard on the accelerator as the engine sputtered, coughed and died. They drifted toward the trees on his side, nudged against the nearest trunk and shuddered to a halt.

Downrange, the van was stopping, too.

"Get out!" Bolan said. "Clear the vehicle!"

He didn't have to tell Coyle twice. His passenger was out and running when the Thunderbolt spit its third round, a white-hot tracer homing on the Ford's gas tank. Bolan was well inside the tree line when it blew, but he still felt the roiling heat.

When he could see the road through a drifting pall of smoke, the van was gone. He'd hoped the skinheads might come back to finish him and Coyle, make sure they'd done the job correctly, but his quarry had escaped.

Again.

"I take it that's the Thunderbolt," Coyle said, fanning his way through the smoke screen.

"What was your first clue?"

"Funny. I let 'em have it, when they stopped to blow the car. I think I hit one of them."

"Either way, it didn't slow them down," Bolan replied.

"Dammit! I don't believe this shit."

"Believe it."

"Anyway," Coyle said, "we're not done yet."

Bolan stepped up to focus on his eyes, the smoke be damned. "What do you mean?"

"You count me out too soon. I've still got one ace up my sleeve," Coyle said, grinning.

"Which is?"

"I'll tell you all about it on our way back to the car."

"Okay," Coyle said. "This guy I know—well, I don't really know him, but I know where you can find him—is a huge supporter of the ARM. We're talking bucks enough to keep the whole damned thing afloat when times are lean. You follow me?"

"I'm listening," Bolan said, as he stripped his combat gear and stowed it in the rental's trunk.

"His name is Arvid Castleton. Don't ask me why his parents called him that. Maybe it's pissed him off since kindergarten and he wants to take it out on everybody else."

"Is there a bottom line?" Bolan asked.

"Coming up," Coyle promised him. "This guy has money from tobacco, oil, a bit of everything. If it pollutes or poisons people, Arvid's got a piece of it and banks the proceeds. If he's not Fortune 500, it's because he's such a recluse that nobody's noticed him."

"And he bankrolls the ARM?"

"Big-time. I plan a whole installment on him for the series."

"It's a series now?"

Coyle winked. "At least. This guy's a closet Nazi, dig it? I can't tell you when he lost his mind, exactly, but he's been supporting fringe groups on the sly ever since he came into his trust fund inheritance, twenty-odd years ago. He uses bagmen, sets up paper companies, whatever. Back around the time of Oklahoma City, CNN broke a story that he'd given six figures to the Midwestern Militia, but someone at headquarters spiked it without follow-ups. I've documented contributions to a half-dozen Klan and neo-Nazi factions in the past ten years, but lately he's been concentrating on the ARM."

"So, Walgren's got a sugar daddy," Bolan said. "Explain how that helps me."

"Helps *us*," Coyle said, correcting him. "Because old Arvid won't just sign a check. He wants to be hands-on—or make-believe, at least. He stays in touch for briefings. Doesn't tell them what to do, but likes to know what's happening."

"And you believe they'd talk to him about the Thunderbolt?" The notion seemed ridiculous to Bolan, as he slid into the driver's seat.

"Now that we know it's real," Coyle said, "I think he may have helped them get it."

Bolan turned to face the journalist, frowning. "What do you mean?"

"You remember that Mexican trip we talked about, where Walgren did his split-personality number?"

"I do."

"Well, rumor has it that he crossed the border for a meeting with some gentlemen of Arab persuasion. The kind who share an affinity for Jew-bashing."

"So?"

"So, Arvid Castleton's ass-deep in Arabs from the petro biz. He used to have Iraqi friends. Now it's mostly Saudis. Anyway, I'm thinking maybe he provided introductions all around."

Bolan turned the ignition key. "Let's say you're right. What's the connection to the Thunderbolt?"

"Come on! I surf the Web, man, just like everybody else. You think I never heard about the Baghdad incident?"

Watching the rearview mirror as he backed out of the barn, Bolan asked Coyle, "Which incident is that?"

"You're playing dumb now? How about a U.S. tank drilled through-and-through by who-knows-what? That ring a bell? I filed it and forgot it at the time, but after what we've just been through, I figure, what the hell?"

"Let's say you're right, across the board," Bolan replied.

"That's what I like to hear!"

"I say again, so what? You think Walgren would brief this armchair Führer on the details of his plans and movements, where to find the supergun at any given time? I grant you, he's unbalanced, but I don't think Walgren is a total idiot."

"I didn't mention any detailed movements," Coyle replied. "As for his plans, maybe a list of likely targets, I suspect we've got a fifty-fifty chance."

Bolan was still considering that prospect when they reached the county highway, heading west, with no clear destination fixed in mind. He didn't share Coyle's confidence that Walgren would regale his secret financier with battle plans and thereby risk a fatal leak. At the same time, however, Bolan was fresh out of leads. If he rejected an approach to Arvid Castleton, his sole recourse was to find Walgren, snatch him from beneath the noses of his bodyguards and grill the man himself.

"You know where Daddy Warbucks lives?" Bolan asked.

"War bucks, I like it," Coyle replied. "We passed him, driving up from Nellie's place. He's proud to be an Okie from Muskogee."

It's a small world, Bolan thought, and asked, "I don't suppose you have his address?"

"Not the number, but I've seen his place. It's hard to miss."

"Security?"

Coyle shrugged. "Technology's not really my forte, know what I'm saying? I drove by the place a couple times, is all. He's got a red-brick wall around the property, looked like it's eight-to-ten feet tall, with wrought-iron gates. I don't remember any guards, barbed wire, or anything like that. I only got a quick glimpse of the house. White columns, like an old plantation."

"You've thought about it, though," Bolan observed.

"Hell, yes. Daydreaming interviews." Coyle thrust an imaginary microphone toward Bolan's face. "And while we're on the subject, Mr. Castleton, exactly how long have you been a raving Nazi lunatic?"

"That sounds like Pulitzer material, all right."

"I live in hope," Coyle said.

Bolan was skeptical in the extreme, but he was also running out of time. Wherever Walgren's men had gone, hauling the Thunderbolt along, he knew they weren't duck hunting. They would want to leave a mark, glaring and unmistakable.

Scorched earth.

If Coyle was wrong, it might turn out to be disastrous, Bolan realized. Instead of tracking Walgren, they'd have squandered precious time and energy on a bizarre dead-end. But if Coyle's hunch was right...

"Okay," he said at last. "Let's pay a visit to the moneyman."

IT HAD BEEN EASY, getting in. Bolan was surprised at just *how* easy, still not trusting it, but he'd been double-checking every step along the way.

There'd been no barbed wire on the fence, no cameras, no guards or dogs watching the grounds of Arvid Castleton's estate. The house was locked up tight, but there was no alarm tape on the first-floor window they had jimmied, and they met no servants as they followed lights and sounds through darkened rooms to find their quarry sitting in a private theater of sorts, watching an old newsreel of Adolf Hitler. He'd been sitting on a sofa with a highly realistic sex doll, both of them dressed up in Nazi uniforms.

It didn't get much freakier than that.

"Who are you?" Castleton inquired, as the Executioner held the pistol to his head.

"That's not important," Bolan answered. Bending forward while the gun stayed where it was, he switched off the TV, then drew an ornate dagger from the would-be Nazi's belt and tossed it aimlessly behind him.

"I must disagree," Castleton said. "When armed intruders penetrate my home, I have a perfect right to ask their names."

"Speaking of penetration," Coyle remarked, "what's up with Nazi babe, there?"

"Your humor is most definitely not appreciated," Castleton replied.

Bolan withdrew the pistol, and they walked around the couch from opposite directions, winding up in front of Castleton and his silicone girlfriend.

"You need to lighten up, Arvid," Coyle said. "The situation has its funny side."

"Enough," Bolan said. "We're not here to talk about your sex life or your taste in videos."

"Indeed?" Despite his evident alarm, the red-faced millionaire maintained a cool aristocratic edge. "Why are you here?"

Bolan ignored the question, responding with one of his own. "Is there anyone else in the house?"

"We're alone," the faux SS officer replied. "I don't use live-in servants."

Coyle studied the sex doll and bit his tongue to keep from interrupting. The big man had the floor, and with a pistol in his hand, he wasn't one to interrupt unnecessarily.

"We need to have a word with you about the ARM," Bolan said.

Castleton feigned misunderstanding, raising first one arm and then the other, smiling vapidly, as if to say, which one? "You needn't spell the words," he said. "I can assure you that my lovely friend is most discreet."

"Let's just make sure." As Bolan spoke, he turned and fired a round into the sex toy's smooth left cheek, snapping its head hard to the left and knocking off its Nazi cap.

Castleton vaulted to his feet, fists clenched. "God damn you! How dare—"

The weapon's muzzle pressed against his forehead silenced him, before he could complete the outraged question. Slowly, inch by inch, his fists and body started to relax.

"Sit down," Bolan instructed him, waiting until the million-aire obeyed. "Now listen up. Unless you want a facial like your girlfriend, there, you'll answer any questions straightaway and save the comedy routine for someone with a sense of humor. Got it?"

"As you say."

"All right. The ARM. You give them money, true or false?"

"That's true."

"Substantial money?"

"By their standards, yes."

"Give me a ballpark figure," Bolan said.

"Last year, I'd guess that it was thirty-five or forty thousand."

"And you keep in touch with Walgren on the side."

"I speak to him sometimes, of course."

"He fills you in on what the party's doing, this and that."

Bolan was making statements, not asking questions. The man on the couch nodded. "Sometimes. Irregularly, I must say. I certainly don't know—"

"Let's talk about the Thunderbolt," Bolan said.

"What?"

Coyle studied Arvid's face, couldn't decide if he was actually confused or simply faking it.

"You put Walgren in touch with someone from the Middle East," Bolan suggested. "They, in turn, provided him with something special for his arsenal. It's only natural that you'd want updates on their progress with a thing like that. I mean, you set it up and pay most of the bills. Why wouldn't Walgren tell you what's on tap?"

"I don't...he hasn't..."

Bolan stepped in closer to the couch and pressed his gun against the sex doll's head. "First her, then you. Answer, or say goodbye."

"Yes, God, don't shoot!" Tears streamed down Arvid's homely face. "He tells me, sometimes! Yes!"

"About the mission in Ohio?"

"Not specifically," Castleton said. "He told me they were off to 'crack a piggy bank.' I didn't know details until he called me, afterward. Of course, I saw the story on the news."

Coyle felt a stab of disappointment. If the old fart only got his news after the fact—

"The next one's different, though," Bolan suggested. "It's meant to set an example, not fatten the purse."

Castleton blinked. "How do you know?"

"I think you may have had some input on the choice of targets," Bolan said, forging ahead. "And why not, after all you've done to help the movement through the years. I'm sure Walgren would value your advice."

"He doesn't have the strongest sense of history, sometimes," the rich man grudgingly acknowledged.

"So, you helped him out."

"It was a small suggestion, really, and I had to spell it out for him."

"The name?" Coyle asked.

"The *reason* for my choice. If Curt was older, or if he applied himself to studying the movement's roots in the U.S., he would've understood at once."

"Someplace significant," Bolan said.

"Yes!"

"Symbolic."

"Absolutely!"

"That's the name we need."

"You want me to betray the cause I've followed all my life?" asked Castleton.

"Unless you want that life to end within the next five seconds," the Executioner told him.

"It's a sad day in America when—"

"We have lots of sad days in America," Bolan said. "Your kind cause a fair share of them, and I'm trying to prevent one now. If you won't help, I can't think of a single reason you should live."

"I don't—"

"You've got a count of five," Bolan informed him. "One."

"You barge into my home and—"

"Two."

"—expect me to surrender the beliefs I've held since I was—"

"Three."

Castleton broke down and sobbed, the padded shoulders of his SS tunic jerking as he tried to catch his breath. His hands were clasped, white-knuckled, in his lap, as he hunched forward, keening.

"Four."

"*Skokie!*" he wailed, raising his hands as if their pallid flesh would stop a bullet hurtling toward his face.

"Skokie?" Coyle frowned. "What's Skokie?"

"Later," Bolan said. "I need to make a call."

14

"I need another lift," the Executioner told Hal Brognola, speaking on his private line.

Brognola took the news in stride. He'd been expecting it, as Bolan tracked the ARM across the country, seeking out the supergun its members might or might not have. "Where to?" he asked.

"The closest airstrip you can find to Skokie, Illinois."

"From where?"

"Right now, I'm in Muskogee, Oklahoma."

"Yee-haw. Should I ask?"

"Get the itinerary, first," Bolan replied.

"Okay. You've got an Army ammunition plant outside Mc-Alester. That's fifty miles or so southwest of where you are, on Highway 69. As far as touchdown goes, I can drop you off at the Chicago Naval Air Reserve Center and have wheels waiting on the ground."

"Sounds good," Bolan replied. "I'll need two seats."

"You haven't dumped the newsie, then?"

"Not yet."

"Your call. What's happening in Skokie?" Brognola asked.

"I've been talking to a guy named Arvid Castleton. Fat cat in oil and whatnot. Ever heard of him?"

"It doesn't ring a bell."

"Long story short, he's been financing Walgren and the

ARM for years, along with other crazy groups on the far right. Maybe the FBI has something on him, but it doesn't matter now. I've asked Barb to take care of him."

"What's his connection to the supergun?"

"He put Walgren in contact with Wadi bin Sadr, to transfer the piece. And he also suggested a target, for maximum impact."

"Skokie?"

"That's the word."

"They never learn," Brognola said.

"You got that right."

"I should do something," Brognola said. "Tip the Bureau or the local cops. Something."

"I don't have a specific target yet," Bolan replied. "We've had so many red and orange alerts the past few years, it wouldn't mean a thing without details."

"I'll see what I can pin down while you're airborne," the big Fed suggested.

"Good. Addresses for the major synagogues and Jewish centers. Anything that's going on right now, some kind of festival or holiday, that might upset the 'Master Race'."

"There's nothing on the calendar," Brognola said, checking the small one on his desk, "but I can make some calls. I'll check on visitors at the same time. Somebody on a lecture tour, whatever."

"Right. You want to send somebody out to sweep the sugar daddy's place, they might find something that will help connect the dots. Sounds like he's been bankrolling fringe groups for years."

"Some people, huh."

"Some people."

"Anyway, I'll set your flight, first thing, then hit the rest of it. If you need anything in Skokie, give a shout."

"Will do."

The line went dead, and Brognola dropped the receiver back into its place. He found a number in his Rolodex and made another call, confirmed details of Bolan's one-way flight within five minutes flat.

That's something, anyway, he thought, as he began to search for contact numbers in Chicago and environs. He had no one in suburban Skokie proper on his network, but there would be someone in the Windy City who could help him in a time of need.

He started with the FBI and kept it vague, requesting general information on any recent agitation or threats against specific elements of the Jewish community. Chicago's assistant agent-in-charge hemmed and hawed, doing his best to milk Brognola for information, while imparting precious little of any value. It was the Bureau way, and Brognola hung up feeling that he had wasted precious time.

His second call was to a local leader of the Anti-Defamation League, a section of B'nai B'rith that monitored hate groups across the country and abroad. They talked about the general atmosphere in Skokie, recent hate crimes in the area, but none of it seemed relevant.

At last, his contact in Chicago said, "Assuming they need any cause, there's only one thing I can think off that would set the skinheads off, right now."

"What's that?" Brognola asked.

He sat and listened to the answer while a knot formed in his gut. After a brief delay, he managed to obtain an address and specific times. When he rang off, with thanks, Brognola knew he'd left his contact worried, but he couldn't help that now. Worry was perfectly appropriate.

It might even save lives.

He thought about the target, knowing he could tip the cops and Bureau now, but something stayed his hand. Mack Bolan was on the case, and once Brognola clarified the target for him, no one could do any more to stop whatever action Walgren's group had in mind. The normal run of law-enforcement agents were constrained, in fact, by rules and regulations that would give their adversaries an advantage in the early stages of a confrontation. Dealing with fanatics who would stop at nothing, those who carried badges with their guns were still bound by the book.

That was a handicap Bolan didn't share, and Brognola hoped that the soldier's edge would be enough to make the difference, perhaps prevent a massacre.

If not—

Then he would live with the decision he had made, one in a long line of decisions that had led to death and suffering for people he had never met.

It came with Hal Brognola's job.

Which somehow, in that moment, didn't help at all.

15

"So, what's the scoop on Skokie?" Coyle inquired when they were safely airborne, winging northward in the belly of an Army transport plane. "I never heard of it."

"I thought you studied neo-Nazi groups," Bolan replied.

"I do. So what?"

It wasn't Bolan's style to sigh, but he came close. "Skokie is a Chicago suburb, north of town. It's population is predominately Jewish. Many of the older residents are Holocaust survivors who were in the camps as children, later immigrating to the States."

"Sounds like Miami Beach without the sunshine," Coyle remarked.

Bolan ignored him and continued with his story. "Back in 1970-something, a Chicago-based Nazi group hatched the bright idea to march through Skokie on Hitler's birthday. They ran into a city ordinance that banned political parades and started screaming that their rights were being violated. The fight dragged on in court for over a year, before Chicago politicians compromised and let the Nazis use a park downtown. They never marched in Skokie, but they got a lot of free publicity—which, I suppose, was what they really wanted from the get-go."

"But they never marched in Skokie?" Coyle inquired.

"Not yet."

"So, we assume the ARM is looking for a rematch, minus the parade?"

Bolan responded with a shrug. "Nazis hate Jews. What can

I tell you? I've got people looking for a more specific target, but we've got no guarantee they'll pin it down in time."

"Maybe we threw them off," Coyle said. "Maybe they'll scrub the job, after you got to Hoskins and the other two."

"Maybe." But Bolan didn't think so. He was on another wavelength, trying to imagine how his enemies had to feel, what they were thinking. They were fanatics, wedded to a cause transcending individuals.

"But you don't think so," Coyle suggested.

"No. I think they'll go ahead with it."

"Maybe they'll wait for reinforcements. We could buy some time that way."

"The Thunderbolt sounds like a one- or two-man weapon, once it's mounted on a solid base," Bolan said. "They already have at least four men."

"At least?" Coyle pressed.

"The group we tangled with may not be the entire strike team," Bolan explained. "There could be others waiting at the target, or converging from different directions."

"Terrific. So now we're outnumbered?"

"We were from the start."

"Do you have to remind me?"

Bolan's cell phone chirped twice and he took the report from Hal Brognola, who was sitting in his office overlooking Pennsylvania Avenue, in Washington. It only took a moment to digest the news, and Bolan put away his phone.

"We have our target," he told Coyle.

"You're sure?"

"I'd call it ninety-eight percent."

"Okay. So, give!"

"Apparently, the Holocaust Museum in Washington does road shows. They have traveling exhibits that go all around the country, showing films and photographs, war relics, this and that."

"And they're in Skokie?"

Bolan checked his watch. "They should be setting up right now, if they're on time," he said. "I have the address of the auditorium they're using for the three days they're in town."

"Three days," Coyle said. "That's quite a window."

"Maybe," Bolan answered, "we can still get there on time, if Walgren's people run a bit behind."

"And what if they don't hit today?" Coyle asked.

"We wait. What else?"

"Maybe I'm getting paranoid," Coyle said. "But I've been wondering what happens if we're wrong? I mean, a hundred things could happen. Maybe Castleton was braver than we thought and lied to us. Maybe Walgren lied to him, or changed his plans at the last minute. Maybe the Muskogee hit will make them fall back on Plan B, and go someplace we haven't thought of. Maybe—"

"Whoa," Bolan said. "First, I don't think Castleton was lying, and he definitely wasn't brave. As for the rest of your scenarios, they're possible, but we can only play the cards we're holding. There's no good reason why they should expect an ambush at their target site, but if they shy away and hit some other place, we'll deal with it in time."

"So, you're not worried?"

"I'm concerned," Bolan said, "but there's nothing I can do about it at the moment. Worry is a waste of time that saps your energy and gives the other side an edge before they've ever fired a shot."

"A hard habit to break, though," Coyle said.

"I never took it up," Bolan replied.

"You're saying it's a choice?"

"To worry?" Bolan nodded. "Some kids learn it from their parents, others school themselves. Nobody worries in the womb. They learn it over time."

"And you just missed it? Man, some early life you must've had."

The Executioner reached for his duffel bag to double-check

his weapons for the fight ahead. Another moment passed before he told the journalist, "You'd be surprised."

EVEN THOUGH HE HAD BEEN expecting it, the rapping on his door still made Roy Gellar jump. None of the others chided him about it, as he stood. They were too smart for that, and all of them were nervous since the hit in Oklahoma, losing Gasser and War Child that way. He clutched a pistol, moving toward the door of the motel room they all shared. He used the peephole and reported to the room, "It's him. You can relax."

Walgren stood on the threshold, his eyes concealed by mirrored sunglasses, his mouth a narrow slash beneath his nose. Bad news brought out the worst in him, and it had been a grim three days.

Gellar stepped back to clear the entrance, muttering, "Come in, sir, please." He closed the door behind Walgren and heard the automatic lock slide home.

After a moment scanning faces, Walgren ordered, "Tell me what went wrong."

"We made it to the farm on time," Gellar replied, "but Hoskins didn't show. Somebody else turned up, instead. Two guys, for sure. There may've been others. They wasted Fuchs and Warren, heading for their car, and then came after us. We blew 'em off the road and split. Now, here we are."

"You were not followed?" Walgren asked him.

"No way, sir. We kept a sharp watch, right along. We didn't have a tail."

"And Hoskins didn't know the final destination," Walgren added. "So, may I assume you're ready to proceed?"

Gellar was first to mouth the sacred words, "Hail victory!" He beat the others to it, as he often did, because he knew enthusiasm counted. It would never be enough to simply hate Jews and harass them. Anyone could do that. Leadership required a certain something extra, that would set him well apart from others in the movement.

And today would be a major step in that direction, Gellar knew.

"Where is the Thunderbolt?" Walgren inquired.

"Still in the van, sir," Gellar said. "We couldn't risk hauling it in and out."

"Of course. And is it ready?"

"Stripped and cleaned since last night," Connolly chimed in, earning a glare from Gellar.

"I checked the batteries," Gellar declared. "The laser sight is good to go."

"In Yahweh's name!" Connolly cheered before Gellar could speak. The others joined in swiftly.

"All right," Walgren said, "if you're ready, then, let's go. We'll meet as planned, after the mission, in St. Louis. Thompson, you're with me."

Roy Gellar was the last man out the door, checking the room for anything the others might've left behind. Taking the shotgun seat, he watched Walgren's sedan roll toward the exit from the motel's parking lot.

"Let's roll," he said to Chalmers, at the wheel. "We wouldn't want to keep the rabbis waiting."

"I CAN'T BELIEVE THIS traffic," Coyle remarked.

"It's lunchtime, more or less," Bolan replied.

Their car was inching north, crossing Chicago's northern boundary and creeping into Lincolnwood. Unless they caught a break, another twenty minutes minimum would pass before they entered Skokie. Short of a swerving run along the sidewalk that would threaten innocent pedestrians and draw police like flies to honey, Bolan couldn't think of any way to beat the lunchtime traffic jam.

"We should have grabbed a chopper," Coyle opined.

"I've got a friend or two," Bolan said. "I'm not the President."

Their slow progress was chafing Bolan's nerves, as well, but complaining wouldn't help. It wouldn't clear the road in front of him, or keep his enemies from striking when they chose, without waiting for Bolan to arrive.

He had a scanner on the dashboard, tuned to the frequency used by Skokie police radios, but the traffic was strictly routine. No shots fired, yet. No massacre in progress.

They still had time.

How much was anybody's guess.

"I have to wonder what they're thinking," Coyle remarked. "Choosing a target in a place like this, I mean. Forget about the symbolism. Think about the *risk*. So many cops and so much traffic, can they really hope to get away with it? If this is martyr time, they could've picked a bigger mark. Why not the Holocaust Museum itself, or the Israeli embassy in Washington? If they just want to throw away the supergun and die, why not go out in style?"

"I don't think martyrdom's part of the plan," Bolan replied.

"You don't?"

"It doesn't feel right, for the reasons you just mentioned, among others. This is still a warm-up for the main event, which means they're fairly confident that they can get away."

"Which proves they're crazy."

Maybe, Bolan thought. And maybe not.

Four raids had brought him close to taking out the Thunderbolt, but still not close enough. The ARM still had an edge, and Bolan guessed that they would use it to the maximum advantage if he gave them any room at all.

They caught a break as traffic thinned in Lincolnwood and Bolan had a chance to let their rented wheels unwind. He kept within the posted limits, for the most part, but cut corners where he could and had Coyle watch more closely for police as they approached the target area.

Nothing felt different when they passed from Lincolnwood to Skokie, but he guessed a person had to live there, share the history and hopes and fears of its inhabitants to understand what made them strong—and what made their community a target for a pack of hate mongers whose racism defied all rationality and logic. Some armchair analysts had once suggested that Skokie survivors of the Holocaust might benefit from meeting with the Nazis who despised them—even that they "owed it to the world" to make that gesture.

Bolan held a different view.

For all his love of freedom and the First Amendment, Bolan didn't think that raving psychopaths should have the right to torment decent people for their own amusement, much less as a calculated means of drawing other psychos to their ranks. The simple answer to such notions was a clear, resounding, "No!" And if there was some part of that the psychos didn't comprehend, he was prepared to speak a language they would understand.

Lynching in the United States had ended only when determined lawmen stood their ground and turned their weapons on the mobs of cowards who got liquored up to murder in the name of white supremacy. It was an object lesson that the rule of law would stand, even if it was sometimes forced to wade in the spilt blood of criminals.

This day, he hoped that message wouldn't be too little or too late.

They found the auditorium with no great difficulty, banner signs out front announcing the historical display inside. There was a line of people outside the ticket office, moving slowly as a doorman checked the patrons through and bargained for the sale of slick brochures. The curb out front was clear, a yellow-painted fire lane, but the parking spaces opposite were full.

No old, blue vans in sight as Bolan made his first pass, circling once around the block. On his return, he glimpsed a blue van on a side street—no one at the wheel and no clear shot from any angle at the auditorium's facade—but his examination of the vehicle was interrupted when Coyle shouted, "There! That's one of them!"

Before Bolan could pick out the pedestrian Coyle's pointing finger indicated, his companion leaped out of the moving car, stumbled, then found his footing and raced headlong toward the nearest intersection. Bolan leaned across his vacant seat to close Coyle's door, then set off in pursuit.

COYLE DIDN'T KNOW the skinhead's name, but he had seen that face in Oklahoma hours earlier. Its owner had been carrying an automatic rifle then, trying to kill him and Matt Cooper. Now, the fact that Coyle had found him on a street in Skokie, near an exhibition dedicated to exposing Nazi crimes, told the journalist that more bloodshed was imminent.

He lost sight of his target for an instant, cursing as he shoved past men and women on the sidewalk. Some of them shoved back—he wasn't that far from Chicago, after all—but Coyle ignored them, focused solely on his quest. He had to find the skinhead and—

And *what?*

Coyle had no weapons, and he'd never had a fistfight in his life. He'd always shied away from contact sports, both as participant and spectator. At that moment, however, he was out for blood by any means available.

Don't think, he told himself. Just act.

He rounded the corner and spotted his quarry, some thirty feet off to his right. The skinhead had a cell phone in hand, talking to someone while he stood and watched the line outside the auditorium. Coyle saw him glance up at the banner overhead and smirk. That snide half smile, half sneer did something to him, pushed him forward at a trot that suddenly became a sprint and carried him past startled bystanders. He hit his target from behind and brought him down.

Coyle's flying tackle stunned himself, even as it sent his adversary sprawling. In the heartbeat that remained before he bit his tongue and spit a stream of blood, Coyle saw the skinhead drop his cell phone, gasping as the compact instrument flew yards beyond his reach.

Coyle tried to stand, knowing he'd have to fight, but there was something wrong. He couldn't draw a breath, and it seemed as if someone had switched his legs for rubber substitutes. They bent and wobbled underneath him, stubbornly refusing to support his weight.

Coyle's enemy recovered first and kicked him squarely in the chest. The journalist rolled backward, crying out in pain, while using the momentum of the kick to pull a backward somersault and wind up in a crouch, facing the Nazi. When he tried to stand this time, it came together somehow, and he lurched erect, fists clenched in front of him.

The skinhead scrambled to his feet an instant later, blinking in surprise at Coyle and asking, "Who the fuck are you?"

"A friend of Bernie Levinson," Coyle gasped, still working overtime to draw a decent breath.

Onlookers had begun to form a wary ring around the two combatants, when the skinhead smiled and said, "A Jew Boy. Sure, I shoulda known."

The slur evoked a few protests from bystanders, but Coyle and his opponent both ignored them. "You can smell 'em coming, right, Adolf?" Coyle asked.

"I smell you pissin' in your pants, kike."

"Wrong again," Coyle said, surprised to find that he was smiling now. "Prepare to have your ass kicked by a lapsed Catholic."

"I don't think so," the Nazi said, as he drew a semiautomatic pistol from beneath his jacket. "Maybe I'll just smoke *your* ass, instead."

The first glimpse of a weapon put the bystanders in motion, scattering for cover or for distance as they shouted the alarm well-known to many urban dwellers.

"Gun! Look out! He's got a gun!"

Coyle knew what he had to do and didn't stop to think about it. Analyzing this particular encounter was a surefire way to die.

He rushed the skinhead, arms outstretched, lips drawn back in a snarling cry of rage, before his enemy had time to aim and fire.

The gun went off as Coyle's hand wrapped around it. The explosion stung his ears and seared his palm. He felt the bullet sting his outer thigh before it struck concrete and ricocheted.

His death grip on the pistol kept its slide from moving, stopped it from ejecting empty brass or chambering a live round automatically. The double-action trigger clicked repeatedly as Coyle's opponent tried to fire a second shot, without result. Howling with rage, Coyle made a fist of his free hand and drove it hard into the skinhead's face.

They fell again, with Coyle on top, but this time he ignored the pain of impact, concentrating on the throat mere inches from his face. Still clutching his opponent's pistol with his left hand, Coyle shoved with his right beneath the skinhead's chin, forcing his head back as the Nazi thrashed beneath him, hammering Coyle's ribs with his free hand.

Before the pain could cripple or dislodge him, Coyle lunged forward, growling like an animal, and sank his teeth into the skinhead's throat.

"YEAH, BLITZ, I READ YOU five-by-five. Don't jump the gun and chase 'em off, now. We'll be there to toast 'em, just as soon as I can drive around the—"

Mad Dog Connolly was grinning, pleasantly excited, when his comrade's cell phone suddenly went dead. He waited for a second, listening to dead air on the line, then said, "Hey, Blitz! You there, man? What the fuck?"

"What happened?" Gellar asked him.

"Hell, as if I know, man. Phone made some kinda clatter noise, then he was gone."

"Dumb shit. He probably dropped it," Gellar said.

"I'll call him back."

"Screw that. He told you we've got targets, didn't he?"

"Lined up and waiting."

"So, we roll."

They had been sitting in the van's cargo compartment, with the Thunderbolt, while Chalmers went to scout the killing ground. He was supposed to meet them there, add to the havoc as they passed and paused to fire the supergun, then leap inside the van before they sped away.

But now—

"We oughta—" Connolly started.

"Oughta nothin'!" Gellar snapped. "Get in that driver's seat right now and move this thing!"

"Okay! Jesus!"

Connolly scrambled forward, twisted the ignition key and pulled out from the curb. Behind him, he heard Gellar getting ready for the strafing run. They'd rigged the back doors with a pair of clips to hold them open all the way, until they were released by hand, and Gellar had them set by the time Connolly merged with traffic. The Thunderbolt, safe under canvas, would remain invisible until he threw the cover back and started firing at the auditorium.

It still struck Connolly as wasteful, rolling out the Thunderbolt for potshots at a sidewalk crowd of Jews. They could've done the same thing more efficiently with AK-47s, or used Uzis for delicious irony. The Thunderbolt, for all its awesome power, was a basic single-shot that wouldn't give them an impressive body count—but it would compensate in other ways.

With any luck, in fact, it might bring down the house.

Connolly made the first of three successive left-hand turns, boxing the block. He sped up on the next street, making up time, anxious to find out what had happened on the street, with Blitz. A high-pitched whine behind him told him Gellar had switched on the weapon's laser sight.

Another turn, searching for police cars, anything that might suggest a trap. The cell phone on the seat beside him didn't ring, no callback to complete the interrupted conversation. Was it really just as simple as a clumsy hand, a phone shattered on impact?

Turning once again, Connolly saw action on the sidewalk to his left and thirty yards ahead. "We've got some shit here," he told Gellar.

"Spell it out!"

"There's people running every which way. Looks like someone's fighting on the sidewalk by the—shit! It's Blitz and some guy going at it! Blitz has got his piece out!"

"Shit! I told that bitch to keep it in his pants!"

"The fucker's biting him!" Connolly said. "Blood all over everywhere!"

"Fuck him! Pull up just like we planned. Gimme the angle!" Gellar shouted.

"Yeah, but—"

"Do your job, goddamn it! I mean *now!*"

Connolly did as he was told, matching the speed of traffic that preceded him until he reached the preselected spot. They'd marked it off on photographs, in practice. He had memorized the signs on both sides of the street and noted where the fire plug stood, a marker that he couldn't miss.

"Hang on!" he barked at Gellar, then stood on his brake and swung the steering wheel hard right, swinging the van across two eastbound lanes, pointing its open rear directly toward the auditorium.

Ahead of them, traffic moved on and vanished through the nearest intersection. At his back, or what had been his back, now Connolly's starboard flank, tires screeched and angry horns began to bray in protest. He was blocking traffic, and the other drivers wanted him to move.

Fuck them.

Behind him, Gellar found his target, squeezed the trigger, and the Thunderbolt erupted. Connolly had thought of bringing cotton for his ears, but then he'd had to use the telephone and carry on a normal conversation in the van, so he had given up on that idea. He regretted it as the great weapon's first report drove needles deep into his head on either side.

"Shit, man, it's—"

The second shot was off as fast as Gellar could reload and fire. A third came close behind it.

Connolly slouched to catch the action in his left-hand mirror, as the third shot found its mark and seared a clean hole in the auditorium's beige wall. From observation, Connolly knew it had to be a different scene inside, as blazing molten metal ricocheted and sprayed the crowd, the exhibits, whatever stood before it.

Hell on Earth, and none too soon for those who had it coming.

"Let 'em have it, brother!" Connolly shouted in a sudden fit of glee. "In Yahweh's name!"

16

Instead of leaping from the rental car to follow Coyle on foot, Bolan had focused on the blue van parked nearby, familiar from the recent clash in Oklahoma. Chasing Coyle might lead him to a single enemy, but Bolan's main concern was trying to avert the bloody havoc that would follow if the others opened fire upon civilians with the Thunderbolt.

He had no time to box the block again. If nothing else, he knew Coyle's rush to battle would alert the other skinheads and might well provoke a premature attack. With that in mind, he cranked the rental's steering wheel, stood on the gas pedal and set horns blaring all around him as he whipped a U-turn in the middle of the busy street.

There'd be no time to suit up for the battle or examine the terrain, he realized. With luck, he might be able to retrieve his Colt Commando from the duffel bag behind the driver's seat, but in a pinch he'd have to go with the Beretta 93-R on its own. With two spare magazines, that gave him sixty Parabellum rounds to do the job.

Bolan could only hope that it would be enough.

Reversing his direction, he glimpsed Coyle and a skinhead opponent grappling on the sidewalk, locked in a writhing embrace. Bystanders fled the pistol in the skinhead's hand, while Coyle buried his face against the other's neck, as if to dodge a flurry of left-handed blows.

Bolan sped past the brawlers, jumped a traffic light just as it turned to red and swung into the side street where he'd seen the van. With the Beretta in his fist, he braced himself to block the van, ram it against the curb if necessary—only to discover that its former parking space was empty.

Gone already, Bolan thought. If they were running, meant to scrub the mission, he had no real hope of overtaking them. Each intersection gave him three directions to select from, and they could be several blocks away already, headed for the nearest on-ramp to an interstate highway.

If they were running.

If they weren't...

His one chance lay in the presumption that his adversaries might have guts enough to go ahead with the attack, despite Coyle's interference and the knowledge that their secret had been blown. If they were bold—or dumb—enough to see it through, Bolan still had a chance to intervene.

That meant another screeching U-turn, clipping a Mercedes in the process, its alarm adding a heightened note of panic to the scene. The light was green for Bolan this time, as he barreled through and made a hard left turn, back toward the auditorium and the Holocaust exhibit. If the skinheads in the van were hunting, that was where they'd go. If not, at least he could retrieve Coyle from the street before police arrived.

A heartbeat later, Bolan saw the van ahead of him, coming to meet him. As he watched, it swerved across the eastbound lanes and shuddered to a halt, its rear end pointing downrange toward the auditorium. A second later, Bolan heard the echo of a large-bore weapon, and a puff of flame erupted from the auditorium's facade.

He pressed on the accelerator, racing toward the van a full block distant as a second shot rang out and drilled the stately building's wall. That one took out a scrambling pedestrian before it found its mark, leaving the body twitching on the sidewalk. Closing, Bolan heard a third shot as the gunner in the van got up to speed.

Ramming the van was not an option Bolan relished, but it

seemed to be his only hope of cutting off the supergun's barrage. He drew a mental bull's-eye on the left-rear corner of the van and aimed to score a glancing blow, enough to throw the Thunderbolt off target without crippling his own car.

The impact nearly shook his hand free of the steering wheel, but Bolan rode it out, braking when he was past the van and nose-to-nose with a bus full of gaping senior citizens. His air bag hadn't deployed, which was something in his favor, but the nylon shoulder harness cut into his neck and chest.

As Bolan shed the safety rig and swiveled in his seat to face the van, the Thunderbolt unleashed another blast. This time, it drilled the tour bus's broad windshield and angled upward, its projectile punching through the roof and hurtling skyward, bound for impact with some unsuspecting target far away. Bolan retaliated with a hasty 3-round burst from his Beretta, stitching holes across the van's already dented flank.

Inside the van, he heard somebody shouting, "Go! Go! Go!" The van burned rubber as he jockeyed for a better shot, accelerating toward the nearest intersection. Bolan saw the shooter crouched inside, behind his weapon, and they fired together. The Executioner's three rounds stuttered, while the Thunderbolt roared back in answer. Bolan felt the heat of the projectile's passage, even though it missed him by a foot or more and struck the bus a second time.

Bolan squeezed off a third burst, nine rounds gone, and then his target made the intersection, roaring through a turn that nearly brought its left tires off the pavement. He turned back in the direction of his car, as gunfire suddenly erupted from his right.

"GODDAMN IT!"

Walgren slammed his fist against the steering wheel as he beheld the ruination of his plan. The raid had turned into a three-ring circus, from the moment that a total stranger suddenly appeared and tackled Chalmers on the sidewalk, interrupting his instructions to the strike team. Walgren had been dumbstruck as they grappled, Chalmers squeezing off a single shot before his wiry adversary threw him to the ground a second time and somehow managed to deactivate his pistol.

That was bad enough, the sidewalk brawl accompanied by screams and panic. Taken by itself, it might've played into the master plan, chaos and terror visiting the Jews of Skokie one more time. It could have served his purposes, perhaps—but that was not the end of his embarrassment.

Gellar and Connolly, cut off from Chalmers, had decided to proceed. That much was obvious when Walgren saw the van approaching, more or less on schedule, braking in the middle of the street to line up Gellar's sight line for the Thunderbolt. It seemed to work, and he had managed three clean shots before the next disaster struck.

A car had suddenly appeared from nowhere, charging toward the van while Walgren looked on, horrified. Its driver struck the van, spoiling the Thunderbolt's next shot, then scrambled from his car and started shooting at the van with what appeared to be a small machine pistol.

"It's them!" Jake Thompson blurted from the shotgun seat. "I know these guys!"

"What did you say?" Walgren demanded.

"They're the ones from Nellie's place. They must've followed us, somehow."

"Impossible!" Walgren replied. Yet, there they were, one wrestling on the pavement with Chalmers, while the other traded shots with Gellar in the van.

"How did this happen?" Walgren raged.

Thompson blinked at his livid master. "I guess…I don't…"

"Never mind!"

Walgren turned the ignition key, released the parking brake and pulled out from his parking place, accelerating toward the battle scene a block in front of him. "Be ready with that Uzi," he told Thompson.

"Yes, sir!"

Another doom crack from the Thunderbolt echoed along the street, but Walgren saw the interloper still alive and on his feet, returning fire as the blue van fishtailed and sped away. The yellow pricks were running! They'd regret it if they ever came within his reach again, Walgren thought, but he knew they might keep running, panic, ditch the supergun and try to disappear.

I'll find you both, he vowed. *There's nowhere you can hide.*

Thompson began firing the Uzi when they were a half block from their target, one man standing in the street beside his damaged car, outside the auditorium. Walgren no longer cared about the Holocaust display. He wanted this man dead, together with the wrestler on the sidewalk. Only then would he feel—

Wait!

It might be a mistake to kill them both, if he could take one prisoner and find out who the bastard worked for, why the ARM was reeling from a string of rapid-fire attacks. He had a chance to solve the mystery and maybe get some payback in the process. Walgren knew with sudden, crystal clarity that he could not afford to let that opportunity elude him.

Hitting on the brake, he growled at Thompson, "Take that bastard down! I want him dead, you understand me?"

"Right!" the skinhead answered, squeezing off another burst of submachine gun fire.

"And stay right here, goddamn it! Don't you set one foot outside this car!"

Thompson half turned to face him. "What?"

"Eyes forward! Watch your goddamned man and take him *out*! I'll be right back."

The Uzi burped again, the only answer he received, as Walgren put the car in neutral, set the parking brake and reached inside his blazer for the Glock 19 he carried hidden there. He drew the pistol, gripped the door handle with his free hand and eyed his target on the sidewalk.

It was six or seven paces, maximum, to reach the two men grappling on the pavement. When Walgren reached them, he would stun the stranger, order Chalmers to assist him, drag the bastard back and throw him in the car. If Thompson did his job, the other shooter would soon be dead and they would have a hostage to interrogate.

A bonus that could make up for the ruin of his plan, before he started hunting for Razor, Mad Dog, and the superweapon.

THE BLOOD WAS in his mouth and in his eyes, but Coyle hung on. His enemy was weakening. The blows no longer fell upon his head and ribs with their original fierce strength. A tremor rippled through the skinhead's body, as if he was stricken with a sudden chill.

A fleeting thought of HIV intruded on Coyle's consciousness, but he dismissed it. All that mattered, at the moment, was survival in the here and now. He'd think about disease, from AIDS to rabies, if he lived beyond the next few minutes and had time for less immediate concerns.

Someone was shooting in the background. Several someones, by the sound of it. He'd heard the supergun blazing away, then echoes of a car crash, followed by short bursts of automatic fire. Coyle didn't know if that was Cooper jumping in, or if the skinheads had unleashed more weapons and produced a traffic accident. Another automatic weapon chimed in seconds later, but the Thunderbolt stayed silent after firing its initial rounds.

How many? Six or seven? Had it trashed the auditorium and slaughtered those inside?

Coyle didn't know, but he was anxious to find out. Spitting a gush of crimson from his mouth, he drew back from the skinhead's ravaged throat and found his adversary twitching through some kind of seizure that had rendered him incapable of fighting. With a sudden rush of sweet relief, Coyle pried the Nazi's pistol from his hand and yanked the slide to clear it. They had taught him that much, anyway, before they caught him spying and prepared to plant him in a shallow grave.

Coyle staggered to his feet, just as a figure loomed behind him, uttering a bitter curse. He turned to face the new threat, recognized Curt Walgren's snarling face, and raised the captured pistol for a point-blank shot.

Too late, he saw the automatic pistol whipping toward his face. It flayed his cheek and set off fireworks in the spinning murk behind his eyes. Coyle was aware of triggering a shot, but had to have missed, since Walgren hammered him a second time with no apparent difficulty, dropping Coyle back to all fours.

Someone—it had to be Walgren—lashed out with a kick that struck Coyle's gun arm at the elbow, igniting another flare of pain. He crumpled on that side, not quite collapsing with his knee still braced on solid pavement, but he saw a hand reach past his face to twist the weapon from his grasp.

Coyle tried to keep the gun but couldn't manage it. His fingers wouldn't follow orders from his mind. A tiny voice inside his head whispered *brain damage*, but he shook it off and mouthed a silent curse, lunging toward Walgren's legs with every bit of strength he still possessed.

If fingers were beyond him, arms still functioned, more or less. Coyle clutched the Nazi leader's calves as if he were a jilted lover in a 1920s silent film, making a last-ditch bid to keep his paramour from walking out the door. In fact, his one goal was to slow Walgren down, impeding his escape until Matt Cooper could arrive and shoot the bastard dead.

Cooper.

Where was he? There'd been shooting, regular and super-gun variety, with squealing tires and sounds of a collision in the background. Was the tight-lipped mystery man still alive? And if he was, would there be time for him to drop Walgren, before the Nazi prick shot Coyle and fled the scene.

Hang on!

Biting had served him once, but when Coyle tried to gnaw on one of Walgren's shins, he tasted only fabric. Fairly weeping in his disappointment, he dug fingers into Walgren's calves.

Give him a charley horse, at least, Coyle thought, and almost giggled. Watch out for limping Nazis, friends and neighbors!

Walgren stooped low and whipped his gun across Coyle's skull again, nearly dislodging his assailant. Between the blood that gummed his eyelids and the swirling motes behind his eyes, Coyle found that he could barely see at all. The muscles in his arms and shoulders started to relax involuntarily, resisting his commands that they maintain a firm grip on the enemy.

"Traitors," he slurred, drooling.

The fourth blow slashed across his neck, behind one ear, and Coyle collapsed facedown. He wasn't out, exactly, but he'd lost all power to resist as Walgren dragged him roughly from the sidewalk, through the gutter and across the street.

Gonna run over me, Coyle thought. That friggin' van.

But he was being lifted now and shoved into some kind of vehicle. He teetered on a padded bench seat for a moment, then rolled to the floorboard with a painful jolt. Someone kicked at his feet and legs until they fit inside the car, then slammed a door behind him.

Good as dead, his mind-voice whispered, as the vehicle began to move.

BOLAN SQUEEZED OFF a 3-round burst from his Beretta, knowing that he'd missed his enemy almost before the bullets flew. He'd been too hasty under fire, triggered the shots without a solid target acquisition, ducking back as Parabellum manglers fanned the air above his head.

He didn't recognize the shooter in the Ford sedan, but Bolan could've sworn he'd seen Curt Walgren at the wheel. It might be wishful thinking, hoping for a final resolution to the grim, frustrating mission, but it hardly mattered if he couldn't get a clear shot at his adversaries.

Bolan had been lucky so far, inasmuch as his attacker's handling of his submachine gun had been careless. The first rounds were fired in haste, missed Bolan by a foot or more and barely scratched his rental car before he went to ground. The shooter had improved since then, of course, and he was keeping his adversary pinned behind the car, firing short bursts each time the Executioner tried angling for a kill.

They couldn't play that game much longer, Bolan realized. Police were probably en route to the chaotic scene. The precinct switchboard would be lit up like a Christmas tree, with calls to 9-1-1 from merchants on the street, plus motorists and shoppers armed with cell phones. Bolan couldn't hear the sirens yet, but they would soon be wailing in from all directions, sealing off the block with uniforms and SWAT teams, while the blue van and the Thunderbolt escaped.

The Executioner had never been a fan of self-deception. Every second counted. He might've lost his chance to catch the van already, and whatever chance remained was fading rapidly. He had to break the stalemate soon, or lose an opportunity that could be his last.

Crouching below the skinhead's line of fire, Bolan opened the rental's right-rear door. He found the duffel bag behind the driver's seat, unzipped it and withdrew the Colt Commando carbine. Reaching back inside the bag, he palmed a magazine and slapped it home into the Colt's receiver. Bolan drew the cocking lever back, released it, and the piece was good to go.

But so was his opponent's, as he found on rising from concealment, near the rental's trunk this time to risk a shot. The skinhead had him covered, leveling an Uzi or a knockoff to unleash another spray of automatic fire. At the same time, the shooter cried, "Will you come on, for Christ's sake, sir!"

Bolan had no idea what that was all about, but instinct told him he should crack the riddle in a hurry. Crouching low, he peered around his car's rear bumper, toward the auditorium directly opposite. At first, he saw no sign of Coyle, but then his vision shifted farther to the left, and Bolan saw Curt Walgren dragging Coyle's limp form across the westbound traffic lanes.

Coyle's scalp and face were streaked with blood, his shirt

and jacket crimson-stained. His toes scuffed on the pavement, Walgren dragging him facedown. Coyle didn't move, but Bolan had to think that Walgren would've left a corpse behind. One of his own men still lay on the pavement there, and he'd made no move to retrieve the fallen skinhead.

Stop him!

Bolan shifted, raising the Colt, but Walgren lurched beyond his line of sight, dragging the wounded journalist along. How long to get his limp form in the car? It would be quicker with two men, in which case—

Bolan rose, sighting along the Colt's short barrel, hoping that the shooter might've been distracted, called away to help his boss. Instead, Bolan heard bullets whistle past his head before he saw the Uzi's muzzle-flash. He fired back for effect, strafing the other car's roofline, but he was forced back under cover then, without time to assess the damage.

Distant sirens raised their whiny voices in the background, while the shooter's vehicle revved up and roared away. Bolan was on his feet immediately, tracking it, heedless as wild fire sought him from the shotgun seat. He found his mark and held it, squeezed the trigger with his weapon set on autofire. Downrange, the shooter twitched and fell back through the open window, while his weapon clattered to the street.

Better.

Bolan got off another burst before Walgren sped through the intersection, turning in the opposite direction from that taken by the fleeing van. The Nazi glanced back for a heartbeat, letting Bolan see the grimace on his florid face.

Battles come down to choices, in the end. Soldiers advance, or they retreat. They charge, or bide their time. Targets are hastily prioritized, some spared while others are destroyed.

Behind the rental's wheel again, Bolan roared through another U-turn in the middle of the street and powered toward the intersection where traffic was frozen by the sights and sounds of combat, never mind the changing lights. He had a choice to make, and there was no time for debate.

He turned left, chasing Walgren.

Wondering if he would be too late for Randy Coyle.

WALGREN WAS MAKING decent time through traffic that had no idea an epic battle had been fought mere seconds earlier, within a few short blocks. He wasn't driving fast enough to draw attention, Bolan realized, when they had put a quarter mile behind them, but the skinhead leader seized on every opportunity to pass and put more cars between them, jumping yellow lights as they were on the cusp of turning red.

Did Walgren know Bolan was back there, hanging on? His pace and timing made it difficult, forcing Bolan to dare oncoming traffic twice, running red lights and risking interception by police that he could ill afford. The good news, Bolan thought, was that the firefight had attracted every cop in Skokie, leaving scofflaw traffic violators free to take whatever risks they chose.

Bolan took every risk he could, weaving through traffic like a broken-field runner racing for a touchdown in sudden-death overtime. He didn't know if Coyle was still alive, but honor left him no choice in the matter. Even though Coyle had assumed the risk himself, defying orders meant to keep him safe at every turn, honor prevented Bolan from abandoning the journalist to meet his fate alone.

Walgren was heading south, for Lincolnwood, and on from there probably into Chicago. He would doubtless try to lose himself in the metropolis, perhaps switch cars or find a place to hide—a busy parking lot, an underground garage, some narrow alley. If Bolan let him reach the Windy City, where police were both more numerous and better trained, the race might well be lost.

He swerved around a slow vehicle, tuning out the blare of protest from its horn as he swung into line behind his adversary's vehicle. A red light waited for them, half a block ahead, but it could change at any moment.

Bolan knew he couldn't take that chance.

He palmed the 93-R, fired left-handed through his open window from a range of twelve to fifteen feet. Four trigger strokes emptied the magazine, and Bolan swapped it for a fresh one as his enemy surged forward, Walgren battering the car in front of him as if brute force could clear his lane.

Perhaps he could, if Bolan gave him time.

But time was something Walgren didn't have.

Bolan went EVA, charging the bullet-scarred sedan as Walgren stood on the accelerator, rear tires smoking, trying desperately to shove his way past other startled motorists. The car whose bumper he had rammed was slowly moving, inch by inch, despite locked brakes.

Bolan reached the driver's side of Walgren's vehicle and fired a 3-round burst into the Nazi's profile from six feet away. Blood sprayed the dashboard and the inside of the windshield, Walgren slumping forward, then collapsing to his right.

Crouching, Bolan covered the skinhead in the shotgun seat, but he was dead already, staring slack-jawed at the ceiling, lifeless eyes already giving up their sheen in favor of a dusty look. At least one rifle slug had pierced his throat, clipping the jugular or the carotid artery, starving his addled brain of blood.

Bolan opened the left-rear door and reached for Randy Coyle. The journalist lay huddled in the well behind the driver's seat. One blood-smeared eye focused on Bolan, while the other went its own way, staring at an awkward angle to the left. Coyle's mouth was twisted like a stroke victim's, and blood was leaking from the one ear Bolan could observe, from where he stood.

"You late," Coyle said, thick-tongued and clumsy with his words.

"I got held up in traffic," Bolan said. "Hang on. You'll be okay."

"Don't think so," Coyle replied, his good eye squinting. "Didja get it?"

"We'll talk about it later," Bolan told him.

From a pocket, he withdrew a cell phone, thumbed it on, and tapped in 9-1-1.

A not-quite-phony set of FBI credentials satisfied the first cops
on the shooting scene. Bolan insisted that he had to ride with
Coyle to the emergency room, for reasons of security, and he
would talk to the detectives when they caught up to him there.

It bought some time, but would it be enough?

The ER was crowded, but another badge-flash and a brief
examination moved Coyle to the head of the line. Bolan stood
by while a young doctor read Coyle's vital signs, examined his
head wounds and shone a pencil flashlight into both eyes,
switching back and forth. The doctor sent a nurse to page a neurosurgeon, who arrived ten minutes later.

Bolan was painfully aware of passing time. No homicide detectives had arrived, so far, and while he knew they'd have their
hands full at the shooting scene, they wouldn't miss an opportunity to grill the sole surviving witness—much less a mysterious
Fed who had pulled rank to whisk him away from the kill zone.

Bolan could bluff with the best of them, and he had contact
numbers routed through the Stony Man Farm switchboard that
would support whatever line he fed the local law short-term, but
with so many dead and wounded in a public place, he also knew
that a full-scale investigation would result. When Bolan disappeared, new questions would be asked. Phone numbers would
evaporate, his trail would scatter like bread crumbs in a hurricane,
but no investigator worth his salt in Skokie would be satisfied.

It was a risk that Bolan rarely took, preferring to avoid all contact with police whenever possible, but two things had compelled his action in this case. First, Coyle had needed medical attention in a hurry, expedited by authority beyond that held by uniformed patrolmen at the scene. And second, Bolan had to speak with Coyle once more, before the young reporter went to surgery.

Or died.

The neurosurgeon ran a few quick tests, assessing Coyle's reactions to external stimuli, then ordered the preparation of an operating room. That done, he closed the gap between himself and Bolan, moving warily. The name tag on his white coat read T. Pliske.

"You are?" the doctor asked.

"Agent Matt Cooper, FBI."

"What's your relation to my patient, Agent Cooper?"

"Call him Randall Coyle. I brought him in. The rest is strictly classified."

That put a scowl on Dr. Pliske's face. "Can you at least explain the fractures in his skull?"

"I didn't see it happen," Bolan answered honestly, "but I'm assuming he was pistol-whipped."

"And is the FBI assuming full responsibility?"

"If you mean money, Doctor, you'll be taken care of."

Color bloomed in Pliske's sallow cheeks. "He's going into surgery as soon as we can get him stabilized. You need to understand that he's in critical condition, with a fair-to-poor prognosis. Trauma this extensive may be fatal, and the surgery required to mend the damage—if we can—entails risks of its own. Right now, I'd say it's fifty-fifty that we'll lose him on the table."

"Do what you can," Bolan replied. "The *best* you can."

More color in those cheeks. "I always do my best for patients, Agent Cooper."

"Glad to hear it. Now, before you take him up, I need a word."

"If I can answer any other questions—"

"Not with you," Bolan said quickly.

It took a beat for Dr. Pliske to catch on, then he began to bluster. "That's impossible. The man's barely coherent, and we have a sedative prepared to—"

"Doctor, there are other lives at stake. I don't know if you've heard about the incident downtown, an hour ago, but I can't even begin to estimate the body count that round two may deliver."

"Body count? Round two? I don't—"

"We're talking terrorism, Doctor. National security. Mass murder. Am I getting through?"

"The patient is delirious," Pliske replied, tight-lipped. "His skull is fractured in at least two places, and there's damage to his brain. Even if surgery's successful, there's a good chance that his speech will be impaired. As for his memory—"

"I'm running out of time," Bolan said. "Step aside."

He brushed past Dr. Pliske and a worried-looking nurse, bent over Coyle and met the wounded writer's one good eye. Coyle tried to smile, but it was twisted, stillborn, more a twitch than an expression.

Leaning closer, Bolan asked him, "Can you hear me?"

"Ya."

"You understand?"

"Ya-ya."

"The doctors here are going to take care of you. But first, I need—"

"Big Jew," Coyle said.

"What's that?"

"Big Jew." Coyle struggled to enunciate. "Walgren say kill big Jew necks."

Kill the big Jew next?

"Who is that, Randy? Who's the big Jew Walgren wants to kill?"

"Dunno. He diduh say."

"All right, then, where? New York? Miami Beach? L.A.? Where is—"

"That's quite enough!" Dr. Pliske said, standing at Bolan's elbow. "I cannot and *will* not have this patient badgered when he should be on his way to surgery."

Bolan stepped back a pace. "You're right. Take him."

He left the cubicle to those who had life-saving business there. Just then, the ER's sliding door hissed open to admit a uniformed patrolman and two obvious detectives in plain clothes. Bolan remembered the patrolman from the downtown battle scene.

He turned and moved away from the approaching officers with all deliberate speed. They'd stop for information at the nurse's desk, and thereby grant Bolan some extra time for his escape. He would gain nothing by spinning tales to local cops. Instead, he'd let them chase a phantom G-man known only by name, if the cop from the crime scene remembered that much. When that quest came up empty, they'd hit a dead end.

As for Bolan, he had work to do.

Curt Walgren might be dead, but he had left a private army of fanatics to pursue his criminal agenda. Whether they would try to carry out another mission with the supergun was anybody's guess, but Bolan couldn't simply drop the mission and go on to something else.

Too many loose ends remained, and some of them might yet prove deadly. By the time he reached his bullet-scarred sedan—another chore, replacing it as soon as possible—Bolan knew what his next step had to be.

"SLOW DOWN AND TELL ME what the fuck happened. Be careful now. You know this is an open line."

A storm of fear and anger raged through Barry James, making him clutch the telephone receiver with a cold, white-knuckled fist.

"It went to shit," Roy Gellar's distant voice replied. "We started in, you know, and then these guys come outta nowhere. Same guys as before."

"Before?"

"With Nellie. You know what I mean."

"What makes you think they were the same?"

"Because I *saw* them, man, okay? I may not be a fuckin' colonel, but I'm good with faces and—"

"All right! Calm down, now and remember who you're talking to."

"Yes, sir!" More than a hint of insubordination sounded in his voice.

"What happened to the others?"

"Mad Dog's here with me. One of those other guys grabbed Blitz. I saw them wrestling, but he never made it back. The others, I can't say."

The footage running more-or-less nonstop on CNN gave James no cause for hope. It was disaster, nothing less. "Did you at least preserve the item we entrusted to you?" he inquired.

"You mean the—"

"Yes, that's what I mean."

"We've got it, yeah. No damage there."

"All right. You're calling from—don't say it!—fallback option A, is that correct?"

"That's right."

"And is there damage to your vehicle?"

A snort from Gellar. "Yeah, you could say that."

"You'll need to switch it. Be discreet, no cowboy shit. Then use the maps we gave you and proceed by secondary roads to Safehouse X-ray. Do you copy that?"

"I hear you, yeah."

"'I hear you,' what?"

"I hear you, sir!"

"Stay at the safehouse, out of sight, until I get in touch. You should be there in six or seven hours, with any luck."

"Yes, sir."

"Get moving, now. We don't have any time to waste."

"Yes, sir!"

James cradled the receiver and turned up the volume on the TV set that filled one corner of his sitting room. Headline News was playing more grim footage from the Skokie scene. James had another angle on the street they'd showed him half a dozen times already, cop cars with their light racks flashing, close-ups of the damage to the auditorium's facade. It didn't look like much from the outside, but James knew that the Thunderbolt's projectiles had to have spread incendiary havoc through the place after they drilled the outer walls.

He also knew that he was in charge, and that prospect was suddenly devoid of all appeal.

The talking heads on CNN regaled their audience with tales of "an unrivaled hate crime" that included three dead "terrorists" found at or near the scene. Two hours after kickoff, they'd already scrounged mug shots from somewhere and were running them with names attached. The ARM had already been mentioned, prompting James to flee headquarters in a rush and hole up in the small apartment that they kept for such emergencies. Now, he sat through another recitation of the fallen.

Thomas Allen Chalmers, twenty-seven. Prior convictions for assault and statutory rape. Eyewitnesses reported that he had been tackled by another man, still unidentified, who grappled with him on the pavement and appeared to bite his neck, resulting in a fatal loss of blood.

Neck-biting? What the hell? James thought.

Edward Joseph Warren, twenty-one. A history of juvenile offenses, twice jailed as an adult for assault and battery. Found dead in Lincolnwood, another suburb south of Skokie, in the passenger seat of what appeared to be a stolen car.

Curt Walgren, twenty-nine, identified as leader of the ARM. Found dead with Warren in the same car, sitting at the wheel. Multiple gunshots to the head and face.

"Jesus."

They had discussed the risk of martyrdom, done it to death in beer-fueled theoretical debates, but this was *real*. Walgren and two-thirds of the strike team had been snuffed out in the span of two short days. Now James was in command, with duties to perform. And he, for one, wasn't convinced that he could pull it off.

If only Curt—

The doorbell brought him vaulting from his seat, snatching a pistol from the coffee table, cocking it before he tiptoed to the door. James leaned toward the peephole, closed one eye to peer outside and nearly dropped the pistol at his feet.

He eased the hammer down and opened the dead bolt, all thumbs as he fought the security chain. A moment later, he had the door open and stood there, amazed and aghast, on the threshold.

"They said you were dead. On TV. I just heard it."

"I was," Walgren said, "but I'm back."

"Jesus, how?"

"It's magic, Barry. May I come inside, or do you want to talk about it on the doorstep?"

18

Bolan left the shot-up rental car outside a busy Wal-Mart, with the key in the ignition. From a nearby gas station, he phoned a taxi and proceeded to another rental office, where he picked up a replacement for the damaged vehicle. That done, he cruised until he found a pay phone near a street corner, outside a neighborhood convenience store, and called Brognola's private line in Washington.

"It's me," he said when Brognola came on the line.

"Hot time, you're having," the man from Justice said.

"Getting hotter as I go. Coyle's in the hospital."

"What happened?"

"He got antsy, ran into the middle of it. Took a beating that could change his life, assuming he still has one."

"Which hospital?" Brognola asked.

Bolan gave him the particulars, then said, "I had a word with him before they took him into surgery."

"No interference, there?"

"I badged a doctor and a couple of patrolmen, but I split before the suits showed up."

"Okay." Brognola sounded concerned, and with reason.

"It was clean," Bolan assured him. "No comebacks."

"All right."

"The problem is, I lost two shooters and the supergun. They're in the wind, but Coyle has an idea on where they might be going."

"Oh?"

"Walgren and one of his men snatched Coyle off the street. They're history, but Walgren told him something on the way, before I took them out. The ARM's planning to hit someone called 'the big Jew.' That mean anything to you?"

"It could be anyone," Brognola said. "Spielberg, Seinfeld, Joe Lieberman. Some rabbi who pissed off Walgren when he was five years old. Who knows?"

"We need to pin it down, ASAP."

"Give me a minute, here."

Bolan waited through forty silent seconds, watching traffic pass, before Brognola spoke again. "There is somebody who might fit the bill," he said. "I wouldn't have considered it, except for what you've said today."

"Who is it?" Bolan asked.

"Nadiv Tischler. He's Israel's deputy minister of defense, touring selected U.S. cities for the next ten days. He landed yesterday, in Washington, and he goes on from there to New York, Philadelphia, Chicago and Los Angeles."

"He's obviously Jewish," Bolan said, "but is he *big?*"

"He's big enough, I'd say. A public spokesman for the country most despised by Nazis everywhere, for starters. And he personally ordered many of the state's retaliation measures in the past few years. We're talking leveled homes and rocket strikes into the Palestinian zone, border crossings into Lebanon and Jordan. Hamas has a price on his head, among others."

Four cities, Bolan thought. Ten days.

"There's no way I can follow him," Bolan said. "The logistics are impossible."

"He has the Secret Service with him, anyway," Brognola said.

"They can't stop a fanatic with a supergun," Bolan replied, "unless they know exactly where to look for him."

"Do you?" Brognola challenged.

"Not if we give them four killing grounds to choose from."

"What's the option, then?"

"Get on the line to State, ASAP. Convince them to persuade

Tischler that he should cut short his visit—or just release a statement to the press, whatever's easier. We want the ARM to think they've got one shot at him, and one shot only. Force their hand, and they might make mistakes. If nothing else, we'll know where to expect them."

"*If* Tischler's the target," Brognola said.

"Right."

"And if he's not?"

"We'll know it when the smoke clears," Bolan answered. "There'll be someone dead we could've saved if we were quick and smart enough. We pay them back the best we can, and learn to live with it."

"This is the part that sucks," Brognola said.

"Tell me about it."

"Still, it sounds right. Tischler. They can hit a lick at ZOG and Tel Aviv at the same time. Two birds."

"Where is his meeting in New York?"

"It's actually on Long Island," Brognola replied. "Tomorrow night, he's dining with the Friends of Israel, at a ritzy place in East Hampton."

"Driving in, or flying?" Bolan asked.

"I'd have to check. They have an airport at East Hampton, though."

"Okay. I'll need details of his itinerary, how he's traveling, complete with ETDs and ETAs. Also an address and a floor plan for the banquet hall."

"That shouldn't be a problem," Brognola replied.

"If Tischler's driving, I can track him overland and try to head off any mobile hits from a suspicious-looking van. If he flies in, it's easier. Cover the airport and a short drive to the spot, then wait and see if anybody tries to crash the party."

"I don't know," Brognola said. "If they've got plans in place, a change could scare them off."

"We'll have to wait and see. If Skokie doesn't put them off, I'd say there's nothing they won't try."

"Unless," Brognola came back to the dismal theme, "this whole thing's wishful thinking on our part."

"Walgren was taunting Coyle," Bolan said. "There was no reason for him to tell a dying prisoner their plans. He got his ass kicked, saw one scheme go down the tubes and felt a need to gloat."

"Or lie," Brognola countered.

"I don't think so. He was obviously planning to dispose of Coyle, assuming Coyle survived his head wounds long enough to answer any questions. Walgren's buddy in the car was dead or dying when they pulled away. If Walgren lied, it means that he was lying to himself."

"Or maybe he was so pissed off he said the first thing that came to his mind, such as it was. He hated Jews and probably assumed he was addressing one. Rubbing more salt into the wound."

"Is this a devil's advocate routine, or do you really think we're on the wrong track?" Bolan asked.

Brognola thought about it for a moment, then replied, "I think it's Tischler. Anyway, he's all we've got."

Bolan wished there had been another way to view the problem, but he knew Brognola was correct. Short of a chance discovery that led them to the supergun and any members of the ARM still wandering around the country armed and dangerous, they needed a proactive strategy. That meant accepting Walgren's deathbed boast at face value, selecting the most likely target, and putting all of their eggs in one basket for a final confrontation with the enemy.

If they were wrong, there would be hell to pay.

And Bolan would be forced to live with the results.

He didn't mind too much, considering the things he'd seen and done in combat during his career. There'd been mistakes, of course, miscalculations that had cost the lives of friends and strangers, days when luck went sour and deserted the home team.

Bolan tried not to dwell on those moments, but they were

never too far from his thoughts. They served as grim reminders of the worst that could happen, if a warrior relaxed his vigilance, let down his guard.

Not this time, Bolan vowed, and started making battle plans.

"DO YOU UNDERSTAND NOW?" Walgren asked.

"I think so, but—"

"No buts," he commanded. "We don't have much time to prepare our next move."

Barry James, mind still reeling from what he'd just learned, found himself foxed once again. "We're still going ahead?" he asked Walgren.

"Unless you can tell me a reason we shouldn't."

"Well, there's Skokie, to start with. We just lost two-thirds of the team, not to mention your—"

"My what?"

James saw the trap and stepped around it. "Not to mention that our two survivors are still out there, somewhere, with the Thunderbolt. If they start running, they could ditch it someplace where we can't retrieve it. Or they just keep going with the gun, and by the time we find them, it's too late."

"You said Gellar and Connolly were still under control."

"*Barely,* the last I talked to them. I sent them on to Safehouse X-ray, but it's still four hours minimum before I can expect to reach them there, by telephone."

"We'll wait, then."

"But if they get spooked along the way—"

"Give them some credit," Walgren said. "They're both good men."

Both good and scared, James thought. He kept it to himself and asked, "We're going with the chosen target, then?"

"Why not?" Walgren asked.

James shrugged. "He'll have protection, maybe more so after Skokie. Maybe we should put some more men on it, just to cover all the angles."

"How many can you raise on such short notice?" Walgren asked.

"I had three dozen volunteers for Skokie. Even if we lose half, over how the strike turned out, we'd still have close to twenty."

"I don't want a mob scene," Walgren told him. "It's too complicated. Keep it simple. Minimize the moving parts. Choose six if you can find them."

"Right."

"And get them ready right away."

"They'll need a briefing, once we've picked the target site."

"I've chosen it," Walgren replied. "We'll take him at the first stop on his tour."

"But that means we have to move the day after tomorrow."

"And the problem is?"

"It's too damned soon."

"Excuse me?" Walgren's face was menacing.

James refused to shrivel under Walgren's gaze, but it felt as though a tight fist clenched around his bowels. "What I mean to say is that it doesn't give us time to get the new men ready, or to get the Thunderbolt into position."

"I believe you said the weapon was en route to Safehouse X-ray."

"Right." James nodded. "If they make it there."

"Have faith. Yahweh provides."

"Amen," James said, not really feeling it.

"And Safehouse X-ray lies within a six- or seven-hour drive of the selected target, if I'm not mistaken."

Frowning, working out the calculations, James replied at last, "Sounds right."

"So, one might say that Providence has smiled on us. Although we failed to maximize our full impact today and lost men in the process, Yahweh has provided us a second chance. He's placed us in position for a strike that will astound our enemies and humble them."

"I hope so," James replied.

"If you have doubts," Walgren suggested, "please don't hesitate to say so. I can find someone among those eager volunteers to take your place."

"No, sir!" James saw where the conversation was going, and the end point was a shallow grave. "I know you're right," he lied. "I'm just concerned about the details."

"We'll work them out together, Barry. Just like always."

Just like always, sure, James thought. Except, I've never had to plan logistics with a damned ghost before.

"We're looking at a high-risk job," he said, reminding Walgren of the price they'd likely have to pay. "Some of our soldiers likely won't be coming back."

"They'll be remembered as heroic martyrs for the cause," Walgren replied. "What better way to end an active, virile life?"

"Yes, sir."

"Barry, we don't need the formality when we're alone."

"No, s— I mean, okay."

"The sooner you put out that call for volunteers, the better. I'll arrange the transportation and supplies. We'll be prepared for anything. And with the Thunderbolt, how can we fail?"

James didn't have the nerve to mention that they'd failed that very afternoon, in Skokie. If the boss—his ghost, whatever—didn't have a basic short-term memory, it wasn't Barry's place to pester and correct him. That could get a trooper killed, despite years of loyal service to the ARM.

But James figured he could take out some insurance, even so, if he was sly about it. He could follow orders, go along with Walgren's plan and still take steps to save himself. Stealth operations were his specialty. It didn't take a rocket scientist to see that Walgren had a few loose screws, but James couldn't presume to save the leader from himself.

When time ran out, it would be each man for himself, and never mind the Master Race. Heroic martyrs were a good thing for the movement, but James didn't plan to be among them, when the smoke cleared on another battlefield.

Survival of the fittest was the only rule he'd memorized when he was studying biology in high school. It stayed with him through the years, and generally kept him out of any trouble that a smile and earnest promise couldn't fix.

At least, until the past few days.

It was time to think about abandoning the sinking ship, but he would have to watch his step and give no hint to what was on his mind. *Survival* was the key, and dealing with a ghost changed all the odds.

19

Hal Brognola made arrangements for the airlift to New York, departing from Chicago's Naval Air Reserve Center and touching down at Francis S. Gabreski Airport, an Air National Guard Base located at Westhampton Beach, Long Island. Bolan hoped the near-pinpoint accuracy would give him an edge over the opposition, but he wasn't taking anything for granted.

Not this time.

If nothing else, the ARM's skinheads had proved they were resilient and elusive. Bolan had missed the supergun by seconds, twice, and he was painfully aware what a third miss might mean, not only for the group's presumed target, but for international relations if the hit went down on schedule.

Bolan retrieved his bags and walked two hundred yards to a convenient car rental office near the base. While he was filling out the paperwork for yet another set of wheels, the nagging thought came back to him that he was gambling on a hunch, protecting a presumed target who might not be in any danger from the ARM.

It was a risk, but one he viewed as unavoidable.

It was impossible to cover every "big Jew" in New York, much less from coast to coast. Where would he start? How should potential targets be prioritized? By their celebrity? Political connections? Corporate rank? The balance in their bank accounts? Influence on the media?

Curt Walgren, as twisted as he was, might have fixated on some figure from his past, some private enemy whose stature was inflated and distorted by an age-old grudge. Or, on the other hand, he might've picked a name at random from the pantheon of stars, statesmen and TV talking heads whose looks, beliefs, or mere existence rubbed him the wrong way.

Now that the leader of the ARM was dead, Bolan could not reach out and tap him for a name. He couldn't go in search of Barry James, the heir apparent, either, since it meant another time-consuming hunt that left their best-bet target open to attack.

Bolan respected the agents of the U.S. Secret Service, but they'd dropped the ball before. Dallas in 1963 was the supreme example, but history had nearly repeated itself 1975 and 1981. Two different fringe dwellers, both armed with pistols, had come within yards of President Gerald Ford during his first full year in office, and while neither actually fired a shot, Ford owed his survival more to clumsy assailants than airtight security. Six years later, a babbling head case had wounded President Ronald Reagan and several bystanders, blazing away at point-blank range before the security detail restrained him.

The Executioner knew there was a lesson to be learned from those near-misses. Simply stated a dedicated killer could reach anyone, if he or she was ready to go down in the attempt. Planning and timing were essential, but the human factor—willing sacrifice—made all the difference in the world.

Israel and other states had learned the hard way that security was largely an illusion. Walls and checkpoints might reduce the incidence of violence at given times and places, but there was no guarantee of safety from suicide bombers or point-blank assassins who offered their lives in exchange for a mission accomplished.

But in the present case, Bolan acknowledged, such a sacrifice might not be necessary. With the supergun, an ARM strike team could reach its target from a distance, penetrating armored vehicles and concrete walls. Concealment still provided some security—the marksmen couldn't hit a target that they couldn't see—but one or two shots could transform an armored limousine into a blazing coffin for the passengers inside. Buildings were somewhat more secure, but targets entering and leaving them were vulnerable to attack.

Bolan's first mission on Long Island was to visit the East Hampton banquet hall where Nadiv Tischler would be speaking in a few short hours. He would check the layout, calculate prospective fields of fire and try to pick out likely sniper's nests. The drawbacks in that plan were that he couldn't cover more than one potential firing site, and that his enemies had shown a tendency to work up close and personal.

In Skokie, and before that in Ohio, Walgren's men had used the supergun at close range, from a vehicle. They had relied upon surprise and sheer audacity to make their kills, and only Bolan's intervention had averted further bloodshed at the second shooting scene. He'd have to watch his step this time, make sure the opposition didn't have an opening through which to strike at Tischler or his entourage.

It was a twenty-mile drive from Westhampton Beach to East Hampton, past three other "Hamptons" whose average standard of living made the eastern Long Island a haven for the superwealthy and their hangers-on. Some of the homes were standout mansions, others masked their affluence behind lush trees and shrubs. The island didn't look much like a battleground, so far, but that could change in nothing flat.

Bolan had landed.

And his enemies were on the way.

Maybe.

ROY GELLAR PICKED UP on the second ring, but didn't speak until he recognized the voice of Barry James saying, "Razor? Mad Dog? Say something, dammit!"

"Being careful, sir," Gellar replied.

"It's called a safehouse for a reason. No one knows you're there."

You know, Gellar thought, but he didn't voice the words. Instead, he settled for a cautious, "No, sir."

"Have you had a chance to rest, eat something?" James asked him.

"Pretty much, sir."

"Good. Because it's time for you to move."

"Move where?"

James didn't seem to care about the lapse in military courtesy. "I have another mission for you. It will make up for the last one, clear the books on that. We have a special target lined up for the Thunderbolt."

"Another mission, sir?"

"A very special job. You should feel honored."

"But—"

"I know you didn't think you'd have a chance to make up for the other mess so soon. I had to fight for you on this one, Razor, but we've got approval from the top."

The top?

Gellar wondered what that meant "Sir, we've been hearing on the radio....well, they've been saying that Commander Walgren's dead."

James laughed, a strange, disturbing sound. "And you believe the media? I'm disappointed, Razor, after all you've learned about the Red-Jew propaganda mills. It hasn't been an hour since I spoke to the commander, face-to-face. He wants this mission to proceed. You understand? He ordered it."

"But, sir—"

"Of course," James said, cutting him off, "if you'd prefer not to participate, I'll pass that word along. In that case, all you have to do is stay at Safehouse X-ray with the Thunderbolt until a new team comes to get it. Is that what you want?"

James didn't need to tell him that the pickup team would come with orders to eliminate all slackers and deserters. Gellar had been part of two such operations in the past. That knowledge made him answer James's question with a crisp, "No, sir!"

"So, you're on board? You'll do your duty for the cause?"

"Yes, sir."

"I'm glad to hear it. For a second there... Well, never mind. You know Long Island?"

Gellar had to think about it for a moment. "In New York?"

"The very one."

"I've never been there, sir."

"That's not a problem. You can find it on a map, I'm sure. One of the maps there in the safehouse, for example."

"Yes, sir."

"Good. As soon as we get off the phone, I want you to pack up the van, secure the Thunderbolt and drive straight through until you reach Long Island. Time is of the essence. Understand?"

"Yes, sir," Gellar replied.

"At Mastic Beach, park near the boardwalk. You'll be met by comrades. After that, the only thing you have to do is follow your instructions to the letter."

"What instructions, sir?"

James sighed. "The ones you'll be receiving when it's time. All right?"

Gellar felt foolish, but he managed to reply. "Yes, sir."

"Good man. Get moving, now, and don't waste any time along the way."

"No, sir!"

The line went dead, and Gellar set down the receiver. Connolly was watching him, hunched forward in his chair, a grim expression on his face. "What's this about another mission?" he demanded.

"James wants us to meet some people on Long Island. In New York," he added, for Connolly's benefit.

"What for?"

"They've got another target for the Thunderbolt," Gellar replied. "He didn't give me any details."

"I don't believe this shit!"

"Believe it, man. We either take the gun to them, or James will send a pickup team to get it."

Connolly recoiled, as from an upraised fist. "A pickup team? That's what he said?"

"You wanna call him back and ask him?"

"No."

"I didn't think so."

"This is crazy. Jeez, I mean, with the commander dead and all—"

"James says he's not," Gellar said.

Connolly blinked. "You're shittin' me!"

"I only know what I was told."

"But on the news, it said—"

"Jew news, remember?"

"Yeah, but—"

"Listen, will you? The way I see it, we've got two choices. We either split right now and hope to Yahweh that they never find us, or we go along and do our job."

"We *did* a job, already," Connolly replied.

"And fucked it up, in case you missed the ending. This time, we can get it right. Make ZOG sit up and notice for a change."

"You think so?"

"Either that, or hit the road and spend your life under a rock somewhere."

"You're going, aren't you?" Connolly asked.

"I am, yeah. If you run, you're on your own."

"Fuck it. I've never seen Long Island, May as well go and give the money tree a shake."

Gellar nodded, smiling. "Okay," he said. "Let's roll."

20

Hal Brognola worked the telephones as if his own life was dependent on the outcome, rather than the lives of total strangers. He had never met or even glimpsed Nadiv Tischler, knew nothing of the man himself beyond what was reported in the media and certain files that crossed his desk from time to time. Brognola knew his reputation as a hard-liner where Arabs were concerned, a stance that saw him hailed as a patriot hero by many Israelis, reviled as a terrorist butcher by some Palestinian spokesmen.

The truth, as Brognola had learned from personal experience, most often lay somewhere between the two extremes.

He waited briefly for his second conversation of the day with a cooperative supervisor at the U.S. Secret Service headquarters in Washington. Officially, the Secret Service was "concerned" by the big Fed's report of an impending threat to Tischler, but he couldn't give them names or faces, times or places. Word of a potential ambush on Long Island raised some eyebrows, but without specifics it was nothing federal bodyguards could act upon.

The FBI had been no help. Despite the "War on Terror," their surveillance of militant factions inside the U.S. focused so heavily on Muslims and pro-Palestinian factions that far-right extremists were widely neglected, if not ignored altogether. It reminded Brognola of his own early days with the Bureau, when a headquarters obsession with "Reds" and campus radicals had undercut investigations of the KKK and organized crime. Indeed, prior to the early 1960s, FBI spokesmen had dismissed all accounts of Mafia activity in the U.S. as "baloney"—a strange example of bureaucratic blindness that sprang in equal parts from J. Edgar Hoover's political bias and his personal corruption, exposed only years after his death.

G-men were familiar with the ARM, of course, and mention of a possible Islamic link had set the Bureau beehive buzzing, but the effort was too little and too late for any significant action within the next twenty-four hours. Overnight, known members of the ARM had dropped from sight, evaporated as if sucked into a parallel dimension. Agents who went looking for them came back empty-handed, bearing more questions than answers.

It would come down to Bolan, Brognola supposed, as it so often had in the past. One man alone, bucking the odds because he dared, because he could.

Unless Brognola's supposition was proved wrong.

He'd thrown out Tischler's name almost instinctively, because he was the only "big Jew" on the radar at the moment, in the States. As an Israeli statesman visiting the land of "ZOG," Tischler would make an inviting target for Curt Walgren's brownshirted fanatics—but that didn't mean he was the *right* target.

And thinking of Walgren, Brognola wondered who was calling the shots for the ARM, now that its commander in chief occupied a drawer at the Cook County morgue. Barry James was the logical heir, but his profile was shaky, reflecting a die-hard follower, rather than a charismatic leader. That wasn't carved in stone, by any means, but Brognola had reason to hope that the ARM might be weakened with James at the helm.

If he was.

And if not, then who?

Walgren was dead; that much had been confirmed, despite the damage to his head and face from point-blank pistol shots. Whoever had replaced him, Barry James or someone else, the current honcho of the ARM had vanished underground, and Brognola had yet to get a handle on the leader's method of communicating with his troops.

He'd asked the NSA for help, in that respect, knowing that agents of the Puzzle Palace monitored most telephone and e-mail correspondence in the States and in the world at large. They didn't listen in on every conversation, didn't read each message typed on every keyboard, but they scanned millions of communications for various buzz words—"bomb," "assassinate," "president," and so forth—and focused intently on those with multiple hits. At Brognola's request, the NSA had begun scanning domestic air and wire traffic for messages related to Tischler, "big Jews," the Thunderbolt and other relevant terms that might pinpoint the ARM's strike team.

All in vain.

At least, so far.

Brognola wasn't giving up, but he was getting sick and tired of turning corners, only to confront a new dead end. Somewhere, a group of skinhead killers were preparing their next outrage, craving notoriety and Racial Holy War.

If Bolan found them first, they'd get the war.

If not, there could be hell to pay.

"I CHOSE YOU MEN," Barry James said, "because you are the best available. Know that, before I say another word."

Standing before him at attention, the six skinheads he'd selected seemed to swell with pride. James scanned their faces, repeating their names in his head as he tracked from the left. Jeff Stanton. David Drake. Paul Richey. Arlen Sykes. Bill Jackson. Greg Putnam. All six had proved themselves in action, three of them with liquidations to their credit, and James didn't think they'd let him down.

He was worried, though. No doubt about it.

"As you know," he told the six men, "a special mission is in progress. Now, we've suffered losses. I won't lie to you. But we're proceeding with the mission for our race, in Yahweh's name."

Six voices hammered back at him, as one: "In Yahweh's name!"

"We have an opportunity to strike a target who is vital both to ZOG, and to the enemy in Tel Aviv. One stroke will send a shock wave through both camps and let them know the ARM is still a force to reckon with. It will mean persecution, in the days ahead, but we are able to endure the worst in Yahweh's name."

The skinheads echoed, "In His name!"

"You will be joining forces with the remnants of our first team to complete this mission," James explained. "They've had some unexpected problems, lost two-thirds of their original combatants, but they have the Thunderbolt. With that, and a determination to succeed, we lay our claim to victory."

Heels clicked and arms were raised. The chorus barked, "Hail victory!"

"Be warned," James told the troops. "You will be traveling through hostile territory, in Jew York. You'll be surrounded and outnumbered by the enemy. Weak men could not attempt this task, much less succeed, but you are members of the Master Race. You will succeed, with help from Yahweh."

"In His name!"

James drew a glossy photo from his pocket, handing it to Stanton, on his left. "This is your enemy," he told them. "Memorize his face. When you've destroyed this man, the world will be a better, safer place for Aryans. Expect to deal with bodyguards, Israelis and the federal pigs from Washington. Show them no mercy. Do your duty. Make your people proud."

"Hail victory!" the skinheads cried. "Hail victory!"

"At ease."

James gave them time to scrutinize the photograph, committing the target's swarthy features to memory. When each in turn had studied it, James took it back and lit it with a match while they stood watching. He held the burning photo at arm's length until the flames had nearly reached his fingertips, then let it drop and ground the ashes underfoot.

"Here's where you're going," James advised them, turning to a map he'd thumbtacked to the nearest wall. "Gather around."

They came to join him, watching as his finger traced the route. "You'll rendezvous with the remainder of the first team, here. They have a van. I have two cars waiting for you, outside. Together, you'll proceed to this point, where the target will present himself. Deal with his entourage, and take out the bastard."

Paul Richey raised a hand. "Permission for a question, sir?"

"Granted."

"What kind of hardware are we taking with us, sir?"

"The best we have available," James answered. "In the trunk of each car parked outside, you'll find three assault rifles, the Kalashnikov AKSUs, and three SIG-Sauer pistols. With the Thunderbolt, they should be more than adequate."

I hope, James thought for a moment. "More questions?"

"Yes, sir." Arlen Sykes spoke with a lisp that had delighted childhood bullies, until he grew large enough to pay them back in kind for all the suffering they'd caused him.

"Go ahead, soldier."

"After we're finished with the target, do we have a fallback route?"

"You can discuss that with the members of the first team, when you see them. Use your own best judgment. Hopefully, in the confusion following the strike, evasion shouldn't be a problem."

Or, James thought, you may be dead. "Anything else?"

The six men stood silently before him, seeming anxious to be on their way. James marveled at the nature of such men, battered by circumstance and poorly educated, four of them ex-convicts, now united in a sacred cause. Walgren had taken white trash and converted them to soldiers.

Walgren.

"There's one more thing, before you leave," James said. "You have another edge. Our leader will be going with you, lending his support and wisdom to the mission."

As he spoke, a door opened behind James, and a dead man walking stepped into the room.

"Good morning, gentlemen," Walgren said as he moved among them, slapping backs and shaking hands. "Who's ready to go out and raise a little hell?"

SHORT OF BEING WOUNDED, waiting was the worst part of combat duty. Soldiers trained for action, lived and breathed their readiness to run, leap, fight, kill—even die, if necessary for the greater good—but sitting still and waiting for the first shot could be torture.

Bolan, as a trained and seasoned sniper, knew all about waiting. He had lain for hours in one position, watching for a certain target, barely breathing when the mark appeared and slowly, slowly moved into position for the killing shot.

Patience might be a virtue of the saints, but it served killers equally. Sniping meant knowing when to bide your time or hold your breath, and when to send death's tiny, streamlined messenger screaming downrange to shatter flesh and bone.

This day, so far, it was a waiting game.

Bolan had cruised the banquet hall, circled the block until he worried that pedestrians might view his drive-bys as suspicious, then moved on to find a vantage point that gave him access to the scene without being too obvious. He had considered tracking Tischler's motorcade, but then decided there was little he could do on wheels to cover the Israeli. Tischler had a retinue of bodyguards, presumably a driver trained in various evasive methods, and a vehicle impervious to normal small-arms fire. That armor wouldn't stop the Thunderbolt, but short of cruising up and down the highway with some vague idea of crashing the attack van, Bolan had nothing to offer on that front.

His skill was waiting, watching, then reacting with explosive force when hostile targets were revealed. His battleground would be the banquet hall and its surrounding turf—assuming Tischler was the target, after all, and that his would-be killers made it to the scene on time.

There were too many "ifs" for comfort, but that was another fact of life for combat soldiers. Nothing was certain until the smoke cleared and the bodies were counted. Only then was victory declared, and even that judgment was sometimes altered with the twenty-twenty hindsight of historical analysis.

Bolan didn't know how many enemies were coming, if they came at all, but he was confident the ARM would send enough to do the job. The supergun gave them an edge, but at the same time it had built-in limitations. Single-shot technology would doubtless be improved in time, but Bolan only had to deal with here and now. Slower weapons, regardless of their power and destructive impact, gave opponents time to move, advance, direct their fire.

At least two members of the Skokie strike team had escaped, together with the Thunderbolt. Beyond that, Walgren's heirs had other troops to choose from if they wanted to reconstitute the team. It would be nice, from Bolan's point of view, if only two were sent to do the job, but he was not about to count on it.

Whoever had replaced Walgren as leader of the ARM had to know a larger team would stand a better chance of scoring on the target. They could help protect the supergun, or flank the enemy and try to take him down with conventional weapons if the Thunderbolt spooked him from cover. Either way, more fighters on the scene increased their chances of success.

But only to a point.

Strike teams could also be too large. In that event, movement of excess personnel could give away the secret plan, focus determined opposition where a smaller group might pass unnoticed. When the action started, surplus soldiers could be obstacles, absorbing friendly fire, confusing shooters on their own team to the point that precious opportunities were lost and victory slipped through their hands.

From that perspective, Bolan knew that he should hope for more targets, rather than fewer, but simple logic told him that increasing hostile odds also increased the chances that a lucky shot would take the Nazi group's target down, no matter what defenses Bolan raised.

It was a close call, either way, with no good choices at the end. The warrior checked his watch again and settled in to wait.

21

"We're almost there. Slow down."

Walgren's mind was racing as he snapped the order to his driver. Arlen Sykes responded, "Yes, sir," and eased back on the speed as they rolled eastward, passing Hampton Bay on Highway 27.

"We don't need a goddamned speeding ticket with these weapons in the vehicle," Walgren said.

"No, sir."

Paul Richey sniggered at Sykes's lisp, slouching in the shot-gun seat, and Walgren's anger flared at him. "Is something funny, trooper? Would you like to share it with the class?"

"No, sir!"

"Then, let's observe some simple goddamned discipline!"

"Yes, sir!"

His rage had been a seething, roiling thing since Skokie, when the bullets ripped into his flesh. There'd been no time to mourn his loss, no way for Walgren to acknowledge it among his followers. His resurrection from the dead had been miraculous, a hard slap in the face to CNN and ZOG, but that was all he could reveal to those whom he commanded.

When it came to grieving for the pain and loss, he was alone and dared not show a hint of weakness to his enemies. That would be fatal, Walgren knew, particularly at the hour of his greatest triumph in the war to purify America for Yahweh.

"There's a state police car. Did you see it?"

"Yes, sir." Sykes replied.

They were so close, now. Barely twelve miles from the point where they would find the big Jew waiting for them, though he didn't know it yet. Death would surprise the enemy, as it had surprised Curt Walgren in Skokie.

But his adversary would not rise again.

The Thunderbolt would see to that.

The duffel bag of weapons at his feet clanked softly when Walgren nudged it with a boot, deriving primitive comfort from the proximity of guns and ammunition. His three-man team was not the main strike force, but they'd be ready to support the point men with cover fire if anything went wrong in East Hampton. Whatever was waiting ahead, Walgren believed he was prepared.

But doubt still nagged his mind.

Dying could do that to a soldier, even when he had a second chance to rise and fight again.

Eight miles.

Walgren unzipped the duffel and began removing the stubby AKSU assault rifles concealed there. It galled him to use Russian weapons, but Walgren gave the Red devil his due. Kalashnikovs were more reliable, more readily available and cheaper to acquire than American assault weapons, delivering a punch with their 5.45 mm Soviet rounds. The AKSU had a higher cyclic rate of fire than the M-16, and at eighteen inches long without its folding stock, it was infinitely more concealable, more maneuverable in tight spaces than any corresponding American weapon.

Walgren loaded each of the three short rifles with a curved 30-round box magazine, leaving the chambers empty as he passed two weapons forward into Richey's hands. Both skinheads also carried pistols, and while there was little chance of Sykes firing while he drove the car, Walgren believed in arming each of his soldiers for battle. An unprepared warrior was dangerous to both his comrades and himself—a liability in combat, rather than an asset.

"We're almost there," Walgren said, as they rolled through

tiny Sagaponack. "Keep your eyes open. We're looking for The Espadrille in East Hampton."

No answer from the front, to that, but Walgren hadn't been expecting one. Richey and Sykes were on alert, craned forward in their seats like children eager for their first glimpse of the entry gates to Disney World.

Eight minutes later, Richey said, "I see it, sir! The Espadrille. Ahead and on the left."

"Drive past it once," Walgren commanded. "Watch for security in place, and keep an eye out for the van. It should be here by now."

There'd been no contact from Roy Gellar since they'd separated, for the last leg of the trip, and that should be good news. Should be, yet Walgren almost wished Gellar had broken cellular silence to confirm his arrival on the scene. If he—

"I see it!" Sykes reported, raising one hand from the steering wheel to point.

The van passed Walgren's car, moving slowly in the opposite direction past the Espadrille. Gellar, behind the wheel, glanced down at Walgren in the small four-door sedan and nodded, just the barest signal of acknowledgment that told him they were ready to proceed.

"All right," he told the others. "Lock and load!"

BOLAN WAS READY WHEN the van appeared. He pulled out into traffic in his rental car and joined the flow two car lengths behind his targets. It was a different van, lacking the impact scars and bullet holes from Skokie, and he didn't recognize the driver, but a skinhead cruising past The Espadrille was worth a closer look. If he was wrong, all Bolan would've wasted was a drive around the block.

The Colt Commando lay beside him, covered by an open newspaper. Spare magazines protruded from an open gym bag on the shotgun seat, one handle of the bag secured by the passenger's seat belt to keep it from tumbling if Bolan was forced to slam on the brakes.

The van was almost creeping as it turned right, past The Espadrille's parking lot, the driver taking his time to scope out the facility. His timing was impeccable, as three black limousines had pulled into the lot a moment earlier, disgorging security personnel and other members of Nadiv Tischler's entourage. The man himself had not emerged yet, as far as Bolan could tell while keeping one eye on the van, but he'd be moving toward the banquet hall in plain view at any moment.

As if his thoughts had been transmitted to the driver of the van, that vehicle swerved sharply across a line of slower traffic and roared into a side entrance of The Espadrille's lot. Horns blared, but the driver ignored them, bent forward in his seat, a hawklike profile barely glimpsed before the van began accelerating.

Bolan saw his opportunity and seized it. While traffic in the lane to his right was momentarily stalled, reacting in surprise and anger to the van's aggressive maneuver, Bolan stood on the rental's accelerator and swung the steering wheel sharply, racing around the two cars that had separated him from the van. Traffic was starting to move once again when he cranked the wheel hard right and followed his quarry, more horns blasting and fists shaking at a second interloper in as many seconds.

It was going to be close, damned close. He saw that even as Tischler's security men began to react in what seemed like slow motion to Bolan, some of them crouching and reaching for weapons while others stood tall behind the limos, hands and hardware concealed for the moment. They wouldn't open fire until a threat was clearly demonstrated, but the van's rapid advance had put them all on instant red alert.

Bolan was reaching for the Colt Commando with his right hand, steering with his left, when two things happened simultaneously. First, the speeding van spun into a tire-screeching bootlegger's turn, rubber smoking as its driver worked the gas and brake, spinning the wheel, swinging his vehicle around 180 degrees until its rear doors faced The Espadrille and limos parked outside.

At the same instant, Bolan's rental started taking hits from automatic fire along the passenger's side, safety glass exploding from the windows there, his right-rear tire collapsing into a wallowing rumble as bullets shredded the rubber. Hunched in his seat, he heard sharp sounds of impact before his ears picked out the distinctive chatter of a Kalashnikov blazing away in full-auto fire.

Now it was Bolan's turn to crank the wheel and swerve, trying to save himself before the unseen sniper found his mark and scored a deadly hit. He couldn't help Tischler or stop the Thunderbolt if he was dead, and now, with his vehicle nearly disabled, Bolan realized that he would soon become a target for both sides.

"HIT IT!" ROY GELLAR SHOUTED to his two companions in the van. "What are you waiting for?"

"I'm on it!" Bill Jackson shouted, as he threw the rear doors open, granting Gellar a clear view of the banquet hall and shiny limos in his rearview mirror.

"Ready!" Mike Connolly barked, crouching behind the Thunderbolt and fiddling with the laser sight.

"Then fire, for Christ's sake!" Gellar ordered.

He'd plugged his ears with cotton, so the echo of the supergun's first shot was painful, but not deafening. Gellar had time to spot the laser's red dot on the middle limousine before a blazing round obliterated it and burst inside the target vehicle. He could imagine what was going in there, the instant terror, and it made him smile.

Gellar was soon distracted, though, as he saw a dark sedan racing across the parking lot, directly toward his van. He raised the Uzi from his lap, had one hand on the inner door handle, when someone from the backup team spotted the car and weighed in with a burst of cover fire. Gellar grinned like a child at Christmas, watching as the sedan started taking hits, windows imploding, one tire shredded, swerving in a futile attempt to outrun the incoming fire.

Behind him, the Thunderbolt spoke again and again, drilling tidy holes in the three black limos that blossomed into hellfire upon penetrating the first layers of steel. Some of the big Jew's bodyguards were firing at the van with pistols and submachine guns, but Gellar wasn't worried yet.

He had a job to do, and he would see it done this time, or give his life in the attempt.

Clutching the Uzi in a tight one-handed grip, Gellar craned from his open window, facing backward, and fired a short burst at the scrambling bodyguards. One of them ducked, another staggered, but Gellar couldn't tell if he was scoring any hits. The limousines were likely armored against small-arms fire, but he could make the bastards dance while Connolly and Jackson did their number with the Thunderbolt.

To Gellar's right, he saw more security men emerging from two plain sedans that had ZOG written all over them. He didn't know if they were Secret Service, FBI, or what, but they had the cookie-cutter look of Feds who had sold their souls to the enemy for an illusion of job security. Mouthing a bitter curse at all race traitors, Gellar swung his SMG around to greet them, holding down the trigger as he sprayed the parking lot with hot 9 mm Parabellum rounds.

This time, he saw one of his targets crumple to the pavement, obviously hit. The sight cheered Gellar, even as his weapon's slide locked open on an empty chamber, forcing him to scramble for another magazine. The Feds had marked him and were firing at him now, but Gellar was amazed to feel an icy chill wash over him, replacing fear with deadly calm.

"Just wait, you shits," he muttered, as the Uzi took its load and lay rock-solid in his grip. "Just wait."

He leaned out through the driver's window, heedless as a bullet cracked the outside mirror near his face and stung his cheek with shiny glass slivers. Gellar felt invincible. He was a holy warrior on a great crusade, and even if he fell, the cause would survive without him, stronger for his sacrifice.

He sprayed the charging Feds with hollowpoints rounds, watching another and another fall. The rest were wavering, still firing as they looked for cover, finding none, and starting to backpedal toward their cars. Gellar was laughing as he saw the first one turn to run and cut the coward's legs from under him with half a dozen rounds.

"Come back!" he shouted after them, almost hysterical with joy. "Come back and see me when you grow some balls!"

BOLAN LEAPED FROM THE rental, putting its bulk between himself and the still-unseen shooter who had peppered him with fire as he approached the van. Hot rounds tore through the right-front tire while he was still in motion, and a short burst scarred the windshield from within. A steady, pungent drip of gasoline told Bolan that his fuel tank had been punctured.

Bottom line: the rental wasn't going anywhere.

More vehicles were parked nearby, the half-filled lot a testament to Tischler's popularity with certain local residents, but Bolan wasn't looking for another set of wheels just yet. When it was time to leave, if he was still alive, he'd make provisions for the getaway. His interest at that moment was cover, and the cars around him would provide at least some measure of security when he began to move.

And move he had to, quickly, if he intended to prevent the ARM commandos from assassinating Tischler and his entourage.

Security was on the scene, of course, presumably forewarned, and Bolan heard the sharp reports of friendly weapons, competing with the rattle of Kalashnikovs. He didn't know how many guards had been assigned to Tischler, what they had been told before the main event, but Bolan worried that they might not be equipped to deal with do-or-die fanatics and a superweapon none of them had ever seen.

His dread was realized when one of the limos erupted into flames, downrange. The slamming sounds of gunfire from the van told Bolan that the Thunderbolt was speaking to its enemies, a deadly message that mere flesh and armored steel couldn't resist.

Bolan reached back into the rental car, straining across his seat to release the passenger's seat belt and drag the gym bag with its surplus ammunition from the vehicle. A wild shot drilled the door above him, passing inches from his face, but most of the ongoing fire had other targets now.

He meant to change that, if he could, but caution was required.

Now that Tischler's security detail and members of the Secret Service were involved, with local SWAT teams soon to join the fray, Bolan knew that he'd have to be doubly cautious. He did not want to become involved in a shootout with law-enforcement officers.

But he meant to fight, and take the battle to his enemies.

Beginning immediately.

Moving in a crouch, with the gym bag slung over one shoulder, Bolan eased back from the crippled rental car and slipped between two others parked nearby. A couple of the shiny vehicles within his adversary's field of fire were bullet-scarred, and elsewhere in the lot, alarms were sounding from at least three other cars, discordant sounds contributing a note of manic chaos to the battle scene.

As Bolan neared The Espadrille, the Thunderbolt continued blasting at its armored targets and a second limo went to hell, flames spilling from its fuel tank where a hot shot had passed through it, trailing fire. Bolan glanced up in time to see the stretch car stand on its nose, then settle heavily on a billowing cushion of flame. Two men ran screaming from the pall of smoke around the limo, slapping at the fangs of fire that gnawed through flesh and fabric.

Bolan hoped that neither one of them was Tischler.

Moving on, he risked quick glances toward the van and toward the source of automatic fire that seemed to emanate from two or three Kalashnikovs. He wound a zigzag course among parked cars, most of them foreign, all selected from the high end of the price scale. None of them were safe now, with the firefight in full swing, but he was hoping they might shelter him until he could engage his enemies.

Bolan did not intend to join Tischler's security detachment. No one on the team knew him from Adam, and their first response would be to gun him down on sight. More to the point, they were already scattered, in retreat.

Bolan had other plans, and now he had a target in his sights: a late-model sedan, parked on the street some fifty yards away, with three men in or near it, laying down a storm of AK fire. That car was closer than the van, and Bolan couldn't pass it by without leaving three snipers at his back.

Grim faced, he moved in for the kill.

WALGREN HAD LOST SIGHT of his enemy but knew the bastard had to be out there, somewhere, likely creeping closer to the van. He didn't recognize the man, had barely glimpsed his face in profile, but he knew instinctively that he was looking at a man who still might ruin everything, if he was not contained. If he was not destroyed.

Clutching his AKSU rifle, Walgren scanned the rows of brightly polished cars, wishing for X-ray eyes that would've let him spot his enemy through any barrier. Most of the vehicles were dark in color, but their chrome and wax jobs still reflected sunlight with a painful glint that made tracking his prey more difficult.

Go after him, Walgren thought, but his muscles were reluctant to obey. It wasn't fear, exactly—so he told himself, at least—but caution that kept him crouched behind the drab sedan while gunfire echoed far and wide around The Espadrille.

Walgren looked up in time to see the final limousine engulfed in flame, another hit for Gellar's team. He hoped the big

Jew was inside, but wouldn't count on it. His hated adversaries were resilient, cunning, and tenacious—traits they shared in common with some rodents. He might have to move in close and personal to verify the kill.

But moving seemed to be a problem at the moment.

Being killed could do that, he supposed.

Unlike a cat, Curt Walgren only had two lives, and he was loath to throw the second one away, but now the situation called for action, leadership, a warrior who was willing to assert himself despite the risks involved. Who else was fit to fill that role, except the leader of the Aryan Resistance Movement?

No one.

Edging forward, he surprised Richey and Sykes, both of them spotting targets from the cover of their vehicle, firing short bursts when one revealed itself.

"Stay here," he ordered. "I've got work to do, and I don't want to find you gone when I get back. You understand me?"

"Yet, sir," Sykes responded, with a tremor in his lisping voice.

"Where are you going, sir?" Richey asked.

"To redeem our honor," Walgren answered, speaking through clenched teeth. "Pin down those Feds and watch for local cops. They'll be here soon."

"Sir, if we wait—"

Walgren leaned forward, jammed his weapon's muzzle into Richey's gut. "Be clear on what I'm telling you," he snarled. "You *will not* move without direct authority from me. If you bug out on me, you'll be a hunted rat until the day I track you down and flay your screaming corpse. You hear me, soldier?"

"Yes, sir!"

Walgren turned to Sykes and placed a firm hand on his shoulder, cocked his head toward Richey. "If he tries to leave without me, kill him! Understand?"

The shaved head nodded once. There was a steely glint behind those narrow eyes, perhaps a memory of every sneer and snicker Sykes had suffered from his fellow skinheads in the past.

"I will, sir."

That settled, Walgren left them to it, fairly confident that he would find them with the vehicle when he returned. If he returned. Alive or dead, the two would still be at their post.

But where would Walgren be?

He marked a course across the parking lot, which ought to intercept his adversary if the nameless shooter meant to hit the van, silence the Thunderbolt. It was a gamble, trying to read a complete stranger's mind, but Walgren couldn't strike off aimlessly across the killing ground and hope to find his man.

This way, at least he had a fighting chance.

And if the gamble cost his life, maybe he'd be surprised.

Maybe he'd find a third one waiting for him and amaze them all.

BOLAN WAS CLOSE ENOUGH to hear the spent brass from his adversaries' weapons as it clattered on the asphalt, with a jingling racket that perversely conjured mental images of Christmas bells. He didn't know where that came from, and there was no time at the moment for armchair analysis.

The Executioner had work to do.

Three skinheads armed with stubby AKSU rifles crouched behind the open doors of a midsize Ford sedan, rising in turn to fire short bursts in the direction of The Espadrille and Nadiv Tischler's burning limousines. Bolan had a clear shot at one of them, but he delayed the moment long enough to risk a look from their perspective, hoping he could catch a glimpse of Tischler still alive and well.

Nothing.

Beyond the pall of smoke that rose from burning limos, bodyguards were racing here and there, either returning fire or dragging limp forms from the flaming wreckage. Bolan couldn't tell if one of those still on his feet was Tischler, if he'd managed to escape inside the banquet hall, or if he was among the dead and dying.

Never mind.

If he was hit, Bolan could do nothing about it. If he was alive and well, dropping his would-be murderers would help him stay that way. In either case, the only course open to Bolan was attack.

He rose from the shadow of a Lincoln Town Car, sighting down the barrel of his Colt Commando toward the nearest gunman, who was still oblivious to Bolan's presence. Chivalry had no place in a life-or-death encounter, and he didn't warn the skinhead, simply stitched his spine with half a dozen 5.56 mm tumbling rounds and dropped him to the asphalt in a flaccid sprawl.

The close proximity of hostile fire alerted the dead man's companions, both crouched on the far side of their vehicle from Bolan. The nearer of them was the first to turn, and glimpsing Bolan from a range of twenty feet or so, unleashed a burst from his Kalashnikov. Haste undermined his accuracy, bullets ripping through the Ford's ceiling and body, only three or four out of the dozen coming anywhere near Bolan.

Three or four could do the trick, though, and they sent Bolan diving for the pavement. Before his adversary could react, he fired a short burst underneath the Ford, sweeping the blacktop ankle-high. He was rewarded with a cry of pain, before the skinhead toppled backward, sprawling on his side. For something like a heartbeat and a half they faced each other, peering through the gap between the pavement and the sedan's undercarriage. Then Bolan's rifle spoke again and ended it, a short burst chewing up the skinhead's chest and face.

And that left one.

The sole survivor of the three-man team was moving, circling around the Ford's nose to confront his unseen enemy. In close-range combat, raw aggression might be all that stood between a soldier and destruction, but the warrior also needed sufficient skill to pull it off. This one was driven by a mix of fear and anger, hoping he could save himself with a one-man blitz, but it rebounded against him as he left the cover of his vehicle.

Bolan was waiting for him, finger on the trigger of his Colt Commando, rattling off a burst that ripped his target on a rising track from groin to throat. The skinhead shivered, fired an AK burst into the pavement at his feet, then tumbled over backward, dead before he hit the ground.

Three down. How many left to go?

Bolan turned toward the van, the Thunderbolt, reloading on the move. His next targets were waiting for him. They just didn't know it, yet.

22

A bullet sizzled past Roy Gellar's face, passing close enough to let him feel its wind against his stubbled cheek. Instead of terrifying him, it was exhilarating, stoking fires inside him to the point that Gellar almost felt invincible.

Almost.

He wasn't crazy, even though he'd worked himself into some kind of wild state since he'd started dueling with the Feds. This wasn't like the mess in Skokie, even though the odds against him now seemed infinitely worse. Somehow, Gellar had managed to convince himself that they could kill the big Jew, slip away and live to fight more battles down the line.

The Thunderbolt spit out another booming round, this one directed at The Espadrille itself, beyond the scorched hulks of the three stretch limousines. Seated behind the gun, Mike Connolly turned back to face him, calling out to Gellar, "How much longer, man?"

The question seemed to have no meaning, as he turned it over in his mind. A soldier fought until he won or died. He didn't punch a clock and stop for coffee breaks, or turn and run away on schedule, like some kind of temporary employee working half days at a lousy storefront office. When battle had been joined, the two sides fought until their issue was decided and the victor claimed the field.

"I'll let you know," Gellar answered, leaning through his window to unleash another Uzi burst against the frantic Feds.

But how would he know?

Clearly, Walgren hadn't meant for them to stay and fight all night, while cops surrounded them. They were supposed to kill the big Jew, make their statement and move on.

Had they achieved that goal? Was Tischler dead? His cars were shot to hell and back, but what did that prove? If they didn't see a body, couldn't verify the kill, how would he know when they'd achieved their goal?

Mission accomplished meant exactly that, not Maybe we got lucky.

Gellar had a sudden brainstorm, awesome in its brilliance. He needed proof that they had dropped their target cold—or hot, in this case, with the flames still leaping over there. Someone would have to go and find the big Jew, make sure he was well and truly dead.

"Jackson!" Gellar barked, from the driver's seat.

"Yeah, man." He sat with two handfuls of fat rounds for the Thunderbolt, a slightly dazed expression on his oval face.

"We need reconnaissance," Gellar informed him. "Take a run up to the line and see if you can spot the man we're gunning for."

Jackson was too surprised to blink. "Hey, man, you shittin' me, or what?"

"You heard me, soldier."

"Yeah, I heard you, but I don't fuckin' believe it."

"We need information, and I can't spare Mad Dog from the gun."

"So, spare yourself," Jackson retorted. "Do you see the shit that's going on out there?"

"I see a coward sitting right in front of me."

"You piece of—"

Gellar raised his Uzi far enough to lock its muzzle on to Jackson's chest. Connolly was frozen where he sat, watching the unexpected drama play out inches from his face. Gellar was curious to see if Jackson would obey or try to reach the AKSU lying off to his left side.

"You have a choice," Gellar told Jackson. "Either follow orders like a man, or die right now, a whining traitor."

"Jesus, man!"

"His name is Yashua Messiah! Don't take it in vain!"

"Okay! Shit, man, I'm going. Watch the trigger on that thing, okay?"

At the last moment, turning, Jackson scooped up his weapon and took it along, but he didn't try to turn it on Gellar. He hopped through the open rear doors of the van, hit a crouch and began a zigzag run to reach the nearest limousine.

"Keep firing," Gellar ordered Connolly. "And watch him, while you're at it. If he tries to get away, fry him."

"Okay." There was a tremor in Connolly's voice.

"Say what?"

"Yes, sir!"

Better.

Relieved, Gellar turned back to his open window, angling with his Uzi for another opportunity to make the bastards dance.

MACK BOLAN WAS DRAWING closer to the van, watching his step along the way and spotting shooters from both sides, when a frightened-looking skinhead suddenly leaped from the rear of the van and scuttled off in the direction of The Espadrille. It looked like suicide to Bolan, but he watched the shooter make it to a nearby row of cars, where he ducked and disappeared.

Instead of puzzling out the motive for that move, Bolan advanced. No sooner had the runner vanished than the supergun resumed its blasting at the limos and the banquet hall, confirming his suspicion that the piece had not been left unmanned. He couldn't spot the laser sight's red dot through the swirling smoke, but Bolan saw the hot round sear through The Espadrille's wall with a quick flash of plaster igniting.

His progress toward the van was interrupted when a burst of automatic fire swept overhead, passing close enough to tell Bolan that he had been the target. Flattening himself against a shiny Lexus he gauged the weapon's sound, knowing that it had not been a Kalashnikov.

And that was bad.

The skinheads might have other weapons in their arsenal—most likely did, in fact—but all the hostile rounds Bolan had dodged so far had come from AKs. His fear was that the new incoming fire might've emanated from some lawman's gun. And that, in turn, meant that he couldn't answer the threat with fire of his own.

Bolan moved cautiously, not wanting to expose himself to hits from either side if he could help it, doubly conscious of his need to avoid a killing confrontation with the Secret Service. They were in a shoot-first situation, where his not-quite-bogus FBI credentials wouldn't cut him any slack, because there'd be no time to flash them while the guns went off. The situation would become even more desperate once local cops arrived, confused and hyped up by the sounds and smells of battle, ready to believe that everyone they saw before them was an enemy.

In Bolan's case, it was the bloody truth.

He edged back, toward the left-rear bumper of the Lexus, moving ever closer to the van. It still remained his target, with the supergun inside, if he could make it there before some Fed cut loose and brought him down.

He edged around the Lexus and was slowly turning when a figure rose before him, dark and dangerous. The ruddy face and clean-shaved scalp suggested one of Walgren's Nazis, but the man was in a business suit and carrying a Heckler & Koch MP-5 submachine gun, a favorite with lawmen worldwide.

The shooter hesitated, gunsights locked on Bolan's face, and shouted, "U.S. Secret Service! Drop the weapon! Do it *now*, asshole!"

They stood together on a razor's edge, where hesitation could mean death. Bolan was wondering if he could stall for time, get close enough to grapple with the agent and disarm him, when a startling event occurred. There was a slapping sound, the agent's eyes bulged, and a stream of crimson spouted from the left side of his neck. A heartbeat later, it was joined by hot blood pumping from the right.

The shot had come from somewhere to the dying agent's right, and it had pierced him through-and-through. He dropped the MP-5 at once, hands rising to his neck as if mere flesh could stop the lifeblood pumping from his arteries with each contraction of his heart.

It wouldn't work, and there was nothing Bolan could've done to save him. He watched the agent collapse, legs folding first, slumping against a Cadillac whose shiny paint was smeared with fresh, dark blood. A second later, and the agent's eyes glazed over, switching off the last faint light of life.

Where had the killing shot come from?

Redoubling his caution, Bolan turned and moved out toward the van, drawn by the booming echoes of the Thunderbolt.

PAUL RICHEY FIRED A SHORT burst toward the men he had identified as Feds, then ducked back under cover. Breathing heavily, he turned to Arlen Sykes and said, "He's crazy, man. You know that, right?"

Sykes rose and fired a burst downrange, then crouched again as bullets peppered their sedan. He didn't look at Richey, didn't answer.

"Hey, I said—"

"I heard you," Sykes replied at last. "You better shut your mouth!"

"Are you for real? He left us here to die!"

"We're in a war," the lisping skinhead answered. "We've been trained for this."

"For *what?*" Richey challenged. "Sitting in a parking lot, waiting for cops to swarm around and blow our shit away? Maybe *you* trained for that. I must have missed that day in class."

"You missed a lot," Sykes told him, glowering.

"And what the hell is that supposed to mean?"

"I know your kind," Sykes answered. "Always do the least you can and laugh at them who do the most."

It pleased Sykes, seeing Richey blink at him, groping for a response. He'd seldom raised a voice in self-defense before, treating the gibes and insults from his so-called brothers as "good-natured" ribbing, even when it made him want to scream and smash whatever he could reach. They were supposed to be together, fighting for the same great cause, and it had always seemed like heresy to fight within the ranks over something trivial.

But now, with bullets flying all around him and his leader nowhere to be seen, Sykes had begun to realize that he was running out of chances. If he didn't speak up soon, he might be dead before the message ever passed his lips. And it was too important for him to stay silent any longer, even in the face of death.

Richey had gone beyond the gibes at Sykes's speech impediment, denouncing the commander in terms that amounted to treason. He reeked of fear, the very thing they were supposed to be immune against, and if Sykes understood him, Richey was proposing that they both desert their posts, leaving the others to fight on alone.

"I get it now," Richey said, sneering. "You think he's your friend. You think he likes you, right? Jesus, you're dumber than I thought!"

"Shut up!" Sykes warned him, holding his Kalashnikov in a white-knuckled grip.

"Thut up!" Richey mocked him, face twisted with rage. "If you wanna stay here and get smoked, be my guest. I'm getting out while we still have a chance."

"No, you're not," Sykes replied.

"What did you say?"

Sykes shifted, brought the muzzle of his AKSU into line with Richey's chest. "I said you're going nowhere."

Richey blinked at him again. "I don't believe this shit! Who do you think—"

Sykes shot him in the chest, five rounds at point-blank range, the impact punching Richey well beyond the cover of their bullet-scarred sedan. He left his piece behind for Sykes, lying where he had dropped it as he died.

"Believe it, asshole," Sykes muttered, as he reached out to claim the surplus rifle.

Now, all he had to do was hold off the Feds long enough for Walgren to return and order their withdrawal from the scene. Sykes heard a distant wail of sirens, but he didn't let it worry him. The cops were bound to show up, sooner or later. He would deal with them as he was trained to deal with enemies, each in his turn.

Rising with newfound confidence, he leaned across the Ford's flat hood and fired a long burst toward the federal vehicles. Glass flew and bright scars blossomed on their black paint jobs.

The sniper round took Arlen Sykes completely by surprise, drilling his forehead just off center, chewing through his brain and exiting his skull in back, releasing crimson spray. He toppled over backward, dead before he hit the pavement, with a strange smile on his blood-streaked face.

23

Slowly nearing the van, the Executioner saw that at least two men remained inside the vehicle. One manned the supergun, unloading on his targets with a slow but steady rhythm, while another fired a submachine gun from the driver's seat. There might be others inside, as well, but Bolan was counting on a two-man minimum as he approached from their blind side.

Who should he try to handle first?

The big gun had wreaked havoc on the limousines, and was hammering the banquet hall. Its shooter couldn't mark specific targets on the far side of that punctured, smoking wall, but each hot round had the potential to ignite The Espadrille and burn it down with everyone inside. Smoke curling from the only windows he could see told Bolan that the place might already be burning.

On the other hand, the cockpit gunner had a clear shot at the Secret Service vehicles, a few of Tischler's scrambling bodyguards, and various pedestrians across the street who hadn't run for cover. His shouts and cackling, audible above the sounds of gunfire, signaled that he liked his work and wouldn't be content with a minimal body count.

"Come on, you bastards!" he was calling to the pinned-down federal agents. "Come and get it!"

Sirens, adding background music to the drama, told the Executioner that he was running out of time. No slacker when it came to making tough decisions, he stepped forward, still unnoticed by his target, and fired a short burst through the open passenger's window, cutting off the gunner's latest taunt in midsyllable. The guy slumped forward, dropped his piece outside the van, and shivered once before his body settled limply in the driver's seat.

A voice called from the rear compartment of the van, "Razor? Are you all right?"

Weighing his angles of attack, Bolan reached up and tried the passenger's door, half surprised when it opened to his touch. It was a long step up, the Colt Commando leading, and before he had a chance to use it, another skinhead was upon him, clutching the rifle, cursing as he tried to wrench it free of Bolan's grasp.

They grappled in the space between the two front seats, Bolan fighting silently while his adversary spewed nonstop profanity. Bolan's rifle was the fulcrum between them, both men clinging to it while they flailed away with boots, knees, elbows, now and then a fist withdrawn to take advantage of an opening. Bolan absorbed blows to the head, chest, shoulders, hammering swift kicks into the skinhead's ribs, shins, hips and groin.

It was the Thunderbolt that won the struggle for him, finally. As they lurched from the front seat, inching farther yet into the cargo bay, Bolan had his first glimpse of the supergun, mounted on a tripod behind his opponent. A snarling lunge drove the Nazi back into the Thunderbolt, its stock gouging between his shoulder blades. At the same time, Bolan spun his Colt Commando like a baton, forcing the skinhead to either let go or risk snapping the joints of his shoulders and elbows.

The Nazi let go.

Without a second's hesitation, Bolan swung the carbine like an ax, slashing its butt across his adversary's face. One cheek caved in, the skinhead sagging backward, barely conscious. Bolan spun his piece around and put a slug between the young man's eyes to finish it.

The Thunderbolt stood waiting on its tripod, beside a crate half-filled with ammunition. Bolan's orders called for him to either claim the weapon or destroy it, but the close proximity of Secret Service agents and police restricted his ability to carry out either of those tasks. With no explosives readily at hand, he couldn't guarantee the supergun would be disabled, even if he hosed it down with 5.56 mm slugs at point-blank range. As for escaping with the weapon…

A sudden thought occurred to him. He stooped beside the crate of ammunition, lifting out a single round for close examination. It resembled nothing quite so much as a 20 mm cannon round, though its projectile had some kind of plastic coating that he guessed would either peel away in flight or else disintegrate on impact. Otherwise, the brass casing and primer were identical to any other center-fire cartridge Bolan had ever seen.

He bent once more and ripped away half of the lifeless skinhead's shirt, retreating to the van's cockpit. Incoming rounds flew thick and fast around him as he stepped down from the open doorway, crouching, looking for the van's gas cap.

CURT WALGREN WAS TRACKING his enemy when Bill Jackson nearly stumbled into him, recoiling with a gasp of stunned surprise. The young skinhead was red-faced, breathing heavily, clutching his automatic rifle to his chest as if he thought the piece would ward off hostile fire.

Distracted from his quest, Walgren snapped angrily at Jackson, "You're supposed to be with Connolly and Gellar in the van!"

"No, sir! I mean, yes, sir! But Razor ordered me to scout the line and see if I could spot the big Jew."

"Gellar ordered you to leave your post?"

"Yes, sir. I didn't want to do it, but he said he'd shoot me if I didn't, and—"

"Goddamn it! Come with me!"

"Yes, sir!"

There was a worried look on Jackson's face, but he obeyed and fell in step beside Walgren, retracing his path toward the van. Walgren was seething at the thought of Gellar's insubordination, countermanding orders from the ARM's supreme commander as if he had some authority to guide the battle's course.

A lesson was in order, and Walgren looked forward to delivering it in person. Gellar had been on the brink of insubordination when they planned the present mission, and it was now apparent that he'd crossed the line. At such a crucial moment in the struggle, Walgren couldn't afford to overlook such insults to his personal authority.

Not when he had already risked—and lost—so much.

They had halved the distance to the van, Jackson fairly treading on his heels, when Walgren heard the skinhead curse behind him, stopping short. He turned in time to find Jackson crouching, shoulders hunched, facing a stranger in a suit whose jacket hung askew, the seam of its left shoulder torn. The stranger wore dark glasses, one lens missing to reveal a narrow, nervous-looking eye, and he held an MP-5 submachine gun poised with its muzzle midway between Walgren and Jackson.

"Secret Service," he declared, making no effort to display a badge. "Both of you drop your weapons where you stand, step back a pace and raise your hands."

Jackson was trembling like a palsy victim, but he didn't yield. "You want my piece," he answered, "come and get it!"

Walgren's voice lashed out at him. "Jackson! You heard the man. Lay down your weapon."

Suiting words to action, Walgren stooped and placed his AKSU on the ground. Jackson was turning, staring at him, with the Fed still watching every move the skinhead made, when Walgren drew his pistol in a single fluid move and triggered two quick shots from twenty feet.

One missed, the other drilled his target's abdomen, as Walgren flung himself aside, dodging the line of fire. The Secret Service agent staggered, stumbled, holding down the trigger of his SMG as he began to fall. The stream of Parabellum slugs caught Jackson in a ragged line across his chest and blew him backward, emptying his AK as he fell. Walgren lay huddled in the shadow of a sleek Mercedes-Benz and watched the dead men dance together, twitching from the impact of high-velocity bullets until their trigger fingers lost purchase and they collapsed almost simultaneously.

Alone once more, Walgren lurched to his feet, retrieved his Kalashnikov and turned back toward the van. From twenty feet away, he spied his enemy crouching beside the vehicle, stooped over the hatch for the gas cap.

BOLAN'S PLAN WAS SIMPLE: wrap the supercartridge in fabric and wedge it tightly into the van's gas-tank funnel, with the projectile pointed downward, then step back and detonate the primer with a gunshot. If it worked out, the van would be engulfed in flames, his best hope of disabling the supergun before he fled the scene.

Assuming he could get away at all.

And if it didn't work, he'd still have time to make another wick, light it and blow the tank that way.

Maybe.

He wound a shirttail strip around the fat brass cartridge, pushed it halfway down the spout until it jammed there, then eased back a pace and raised the carbine to his shoulder. It was set for semiauto fire, one shot per squeeze, and one was all he'd get on this attempt. If Bolan missed the primer, or it failed to detonate for any reason, he would likely rupture the shell's brass casing and render it harmless.

One shot, then, and he'd have to make it count.

Bolan was peering through the Colt Commando's sight, leaning toward target acquisition, when a voice behind him called out, "Not so fast!"

Bolan froze where he stood, uncertain who the man behind him was or what he planned. A bullet without warning would've done the trick, but this one had something to say. Was he a Secret Service agent, or a Nazi with a gift for gab?

Instead of having Bolan drop his gun and turn around, the

new arrival said, "You really thought that you could kill me, didn't you?"

"I don't know how to answer that," Bolan replied, "until I've seen your face."

"So, turn around," the voice instructed him. "But carefully. I want your weapon pointed at the ground."

Bolan obliged, surprised that he had not been told to place the carbine on the ground. Surprise turned to amazement as he swiveled on his heels and found himself confronted with a man he had already killed, in Illinois.

"You see?" the specter told him, smiling wickedly. "I don't stay dead."

"Congratulations," Bolan said. He couldn't think of any other answer at the moment.

"Your kind think you can kill the movement with the messenger," Curt Walgren said. "But I've got news for you. You've failed. The messenger is still alive. You'll never stop the movement."

Bolan had no time to consider where this man had come from, who he was, or who had died outside Chicago, wearing Walgren's face. Unless he dealt with this fanatic in the next few seconds, they would be hip-deep in uniforms and Bolan would've missed his chance to trash the supergun.

"I'd love to stay and chat," Bolan said, "but I've got a deadline."

Walgren's mirror image grimaced at him. "You're already standing on it, dead man. But before you go, I want to know who sent you."

"Can't you guess?" Bolan asked.

"What? You mean—"

He nodded, playing to the Nazi's paranoia. "Who else has the money or the influence?" Bolan asked.

"Yes! I knew it!" Still, behind the smile, there was a trace of doubt. "But how'd you know about the Thunderbolt, and where to find it?"

"Well—"

It started with a shrug, then Bolan threw himself sideways, crouching and thrusting with his legs at the same time. He raised and fired the Colt Commando in a firm one-handed grip, unloading half the magazine before asphalt arrested his progress.

The Walgren look-alike was jerking, taking hits, and firing back at Bolan with his AKSU rifle, but his dying hands went spastic on him and he couldn't find his target. Bullets ripped along the drab flank of the van, punched through to end their flight somewhere inside. When he collapsed, his attitude revealed the slack finality of death.

Rising, Bolan spared the dead Nazi one brief glance, then turned and found his mark again. The wailing sirens were on top of him, drowning the sound of conscious and coherent thought. He sighted on the cartridge primer, fired and turned to run.

Bolan covered three long strides before the van's gas tank exploded and the shock wave sent him tumbling through space.

Epilogue

"And you got out in the confusion?" Hal Brognola asked.

"I showed my FBI badge to a couple of patrolmen guarding the perimeter," Bolan replied. "They didn't question it. I think the whole thing had them freaking."

"It's no wonder," said the man from Justice. "Turns out that our buddies in the Secret Service didn't tip the locals that there might be trouble on their turf."

"I thought you warned the Service, going in."

"I did," the big Fed confirmed. "Chapter and verse about the threat to Tischler from the ARM. They analyzed it and decided it was bogus—or low risk, at any rate. No reason to disturb the boys and girls in blue with such a flimsy lead, when they could handle it themselves."

"How many did they lose?" Bolan asked.

"Two dead," Brognola answered, "and four wounded. They're already mounting an investigation. Heads are gonna roll."

"And Stony Man?"

"I'll keep the lid on," Brognola assured him. "Hang a snitch jacket on one of Walgren's men who's not in a position to defend himself. The Secret Service fumbled this one, by deciding to ignore the tip. That's how it reads in my report."

"Tischler came through all right, I understand."

"A little singed around the edges, but he'll live to speak another day. His bodyguards may want a raise, at least the ones who made it through."

"Bad losses there?" Bolan asked.

"Five dead on arrival, three more hanging on by a thread in burn units. Four others suffered minor injuries. They held the line, though. Saved their boss. That's all that matters in the trade."

Bolan was stalling on the question that was foremost in his mind. He wanted answers, but the very thought of voicing the inquiry made his skin crawl. As it was, he asked about the subject that was second on his list of postfirefight priorities.

"Who's got the supergun, or what was left of it?"

"The piece was toasted and the ammo all cooked off, which started scattered fires within a two-block radius. Firefighters doused the van and were the first to look inside. Local police put in their bid to claim the weapon, but a call from Washington scotched that. After some argument, the Secret Service claimed it, then the FBI stepped in, declared the incident an act of terrorism and asserted their authority to analyze all evidence. They're working on it now at their ballistics lab."

"Sorry." Bolan could think of nothing else to say.

"At least it's off the streets," Brognola said. "And pressure from the White House has the Bureau sharing information for a change. We may not have the weapon, but at least we're getting specs."

"What was it, then?" Bolan asked. Stalling, still.

"Essentially, it was a twenty-millimeter sniper's rifle, like a blown-up copy of the Barrett Fifty. Its designer lined the barrel with titanium, instead of steel, and whipped up bullets with a core that sparks on impact or exposure to oxygen. Something on the order of white phosphorus or thermite. We've got chemists working on it, but they didn't find a round intact."

"So, it's a mystery?"

"For now," Brognola said. "They'll work it out, in time."

"Before the next one surfaces?"

"That has some people worried," Brognola admitted. "I won't lie to you. They wonder if the piece was mass-produced, and if it was, where are the rest? Who has them? Why haven't they been used, yet?"

"All good questions," Bolan said.

"But what we need are answers. Anyway, it's not your problem."

They strolled beside the broad Potomac River, passed by joggers, skaters and bicyclists on all sides.

"What gives with Randy Coyle?" Bolan asked.

"The kid's improving," Brognola replied, "but he still has a long way to go. That kind of fracturing, with major swelling of the brain, there's bound to be residual impairment."

"All he wanted was a story," Bolan said.

"He got it. Someone else may have to write it for him, though."

"When will they have a clear prognosis?"

"Hard to say. It's the equivalent of a major stroke. He's survived it, so far, but how much of himself still remains is a question the doctors can't answer right now. He could recover ninety-five percent, or nothing much at all."

"Seems like a waste," said Bolan.

"I agree. But he went looking for the story, for the guys who killed his friend. He knew the risks and went ahead. You tried to sideline him, but he kept pushing. This is *not* your fault."

"I know that. Still, it's not exactly what I'd call a shining moment."

"Those are few and far between," Brognola said. "I'll take what I can get."

"There should be something we can do," Bolan replied.

"Like what? Turn back the clock? I wish."

Brognola had a point. Bolan knew he could only play the cards as they were dealt to him, improve his hand by drawing now and then. But for the most part, he could only raise or fold.

He'd raised the ante this time, and the game was his, but those who'd fallen out along the way would bear the brunt of suffering, together with their loved ones who survived.

It was the way of war, and always would be.

Bolan slowed down, frowning. "There's one more thing," he said.

"I thought so. Walgren, right?"

A nod. "I've heard of using doubles, going back to Churchill and Hitler in the Big War, but the resemblance surprised me."

"That's because they weren't doubles," Brognola said. "They were *duplicates*. Twins."

Bolan stopped in his tracks, facing his friend. "I read the file on Walgren. There was no mention of any siblings, much less an identical twin."

"We missed it," Brognola admitted. "Everybody missed it, going back to kindergarten. That's a story in itself."

"I'm listening."

"Okay. From what we've pieced together, Walgren's mother—Noreen—never married. She got pregnant in her early teens, some boy who didn't stick around. Her parents were religious to the max, the kind who couldn't tolerate abortion *or* a little bastard in the family. So, they kicked her out and wrote her off. 'We have no daughter.' All that happy crap."

"And she had twins?"

Brognola nodded. "Living in a Cleveland flophouse with some kids she met on the street, apparently. God only knows how either of the newborns managed to survive their first night in the world, much less the next few years. Somewhere along the way, Noreen's mind snapped. What we're hearing now is that she managed to convince herself that she could handle one kid, but she couldn't manage two. The answer she came up with was to raise the twins as one. Apparently, she gave them both the same first name—her father's, if you can believe it—and she taught them to regard themselves as two halves of a single person. When you hear it from the cradle up, I guess it makes a crazy kind of sense."

"Whatever mother says?"

"That's it."

"How did they manage school?" Bolan asked.

"You've heard about twins who switch classes or dates, I suppose?" Brognola waited for Bolan's nod, before he continued. "Well, the two Curt Walgrens took it all the way. Apparently, they went to school in shifts, rotating days, and pooled resources on their homework. Noreen kept them home most of the time, hiding her secret when they weren't in school. Then, when the boys were six or seven, Mama got religion."

"Let me guess. Christian Identity?"

"The very same. We don't know if her childhood predisposed her to extremist views, but she liked what she heard and jumped in with both feet. We knew this part, of course, but not that she was raising two young Nazis for the price of one."

"So, they were brainwashed from the time they learned to read."

"While hiding Mama's little secret under threat of punishment at home. The Bureau's interviewed a few of Noreen's friends—defectors from the faith. They recall her as quick with a belt or a fist, at the slightest infraction. Spare the rod and spoil the child, you know? For special kiddy sins, she had a closet, nice and dark. Nearly airtight."

"Confusion and abuse, with Nazi doctrine for dessert. That's quite a recipe."

"A do-it-yourself Hitler kit," Brognola agreed. "One night, when the Curts were sixteen, Noreen's single-wide trailer caught fire and went up like a tarpaper shack. The cops who worked it heard about a boy but couldn't find him. Something tells me they didn't try very hard."

"And they fell through the cracks," Bolan said.

"All the way," Brognola granted. "Living hand to mouth, by any means available. They fell in with a gang of skinheads, but apparently still managed not to drop the ball, where Noreen's secret was concerned."

Bolan considered that, the strength of will and sheer tenacity required for two youths to maintain the fantasy that they were one, growing into manhood with a secret so ingrained that it became a way of life, the way they viewed a hostile world.

"You'll love this," Brognola said. "When the Bureau picked up Barry James last night in Oklahoma City, he kept asking the agents for proof that Walgren was dead. It turns out even he was in the dark about Curt's twin brother. After one of them went down in Illinois, James thought he was in charge. Then, out of nowhere, comes his old friend claiming he's back from the grave. James thought he was living a sequel to *Day of the Dead.*"

"He understands the truth, now?"

"Well, who really knows what Nazis understand? Their whole philosophy is built on various gradations of insanity. But, yeah, I think old brother Barry knows that he was conned by Fric and Frac. It's made him talkative in custody."

"You've still got others to run down, I guess."

"The Bureau and the Secret Service have. We're out of it, unless we get another call about it from the Oval Office. Anyway, the roundup should be finished soon. The big fish are already netted or filleted. There's only small fry left, and if a few of them slip through the net, so what? They always surface with another bunch of fruitcakes, given time. We'll pick them off eventually, if they're worth the effort."

"And their Middle Eastern links?" Bolan asked.

Brognola responded with a weary shrug. "Wadi bin Sadr may still be out there. We may have another shot at him, sometime, but I'm not counting on it. Pinning that one down could take forever."

"It's not our problem, then," Bolan said.

"For now," Brognola answered.

"Right. For now."

There was always tomorrow, with new threats and villains in store. Wadi bin Sadr might return with a vengeance and more superweapons next week, or next month. If and when he did, Bolan might be summoned to deal with the threat as he'd dealt with this one, through a combination of cunning and brute force. He didn't mind. It was the life he'd chosen, no looking back, and while some changes had been made along the way, Bolan had never flinched from carrying out his duty.

The lyrics of an old Sinatra song wafted through Bolan's mind. He had a few regrets, all right, but who would understand or even have the time to talk about such ancient history? Now, Randy Coyle was added to the list, a young man broken in his prime, perhaps beyond repair.

Choices.

Coyle had begun his quest for truth in hopes of avenging the murder of a friend. He had achieved that goal, at least, whether or not his present mental state allowed him to appreciate the fact. As for his story, only time would tell if Coyle could write it, or if it would ever see the light of day.

That thought sparked yet another in the warrior's mind. "About Coyle," he said. "Assuming that he ever writes his story and can find a publisher, somebody needs to have a word with him before it goes to press."

"You think he'd blow the whistle?"

Bolan shrugged at that. "He doesn't know about the Farm. We never talked about who put me on the case, or anything like that. But still…"

Brognola nodded. "But still. I'll stay on top of it. He won't be writing for a while, but I know people at the hospital and in the business. If he starts to shop a piece around, I'll send someone to brief him on the ins and outs of national security."

"I wouldn't want him damaged any further," Bolan said.

"You know me. I'm the soul of patience," the big Fed replied. "Worse comes to worst, we'll find a way to freeze the story out of mainstream media. Send him to *Paranoia Weekly* or some other rag that no one reads."

Bolan felt something vaguely similar to guilt, regretting that he had to scheme against Coyle's plans, while the reporter was attached to various machines in ICU. The time to squelch a problem, though, was early on, before it came around to bite them from behind.

"Maybe he'll write about the ARM and let it go at that," Bolan suggested.

"Maybe. If he writes at all."

Bolan hadn't gone to visit Coyle at the hospital, nor did he intend to. Their lives had intersected for a few chaotic days, but that was over. They were not colleagues, much less friends. There was no bond between them that required ongoing contact. Bolan didn't need a Boswell in his life, and Coyle most definitely didn't need a warrior dragging him around to one killing ground after another.

The Executioner suspected that Coyle had seen enough of combat for a while. If he recovered from his wounds with memories intact, he could describe the Aryan Resistance Movement's crimes against the country and its people. He could tell a story of humanity perverted in the service of a hateful, psychopathic doctrine that required extermination of some human beings, so that others could proclaim a false superiority.

And what a motley crew the "Master Race" turned out to be, on close examination. Misfits. Felons. Maniacs and morons, led by poster children for a lockdown mental care facility. The ARM itself served as a cautionary tale against racism and religious bigotry—but who would listen? Who would take the problem seriously, in the modern day and age?

Too many other problems clamored for immediate attention in the here and now. Gas prices. Unemployment. Foreign wars that may have been a bad idea to start with, but which soon assumed lives of their own. A host of foreign enemies who blamed America and its elected leaders for the problems of the world at large: pollution, global warming, civil wars, narcotics, random violence in the streets.

There might be no solutions to those problems, but it didn't mean that people couldn't—shouldn't—try. And while they grappled with the mega-issues, Bolan would be working in the shadows, fighting day and night to keep the predators at bay. It was a job that he knew how to do, a job from which he never turned away.

But he was finished, for this day.

Tomorrow would be coming soon enough, and it would take care of itself.

"I need some rest," he told Brognola.

"I imagine so."

"You've got my number."

"Right. Take care."

They shook hands, briefly, before Bolan turned and started back in the direction of his car. He craved somewhere to sleep, someplace where he would be permitted to forget, if only for a little while.

Did such a place exist?

The Executioner moved on, in search of home.

James Axler
Outlanders

LORDS OF THE DEEP
Outlanders #38

The turquoise utopia of the South Pacific belies the mammoth evil rising beneath the waves as Kane and his companions come to the aid of islanders under attack by a degenerate sea nation thriving within a massive dome on the ocean floor. Now the half-human inhabitants of Lemuria have become the violent henchmen of the one true lord of the deep, a creature whose tenacious grip on the stygian depths—and all sentient souls in his path—tightens with terrible power as he prepares to reclaim his world.

Available August 2006 wherever you buy books.